813.54 A132d
Abbott, Lee K.
Dreams of dist...

D1201517

DREAMS
OF
DISTANT
LIVES

ALSO BY LEE K. ABBOTT

STRANGERS IN PARADISE

LOVE IS THE CROOKED THING

THE HEART NEVER FITS ITS WANTING

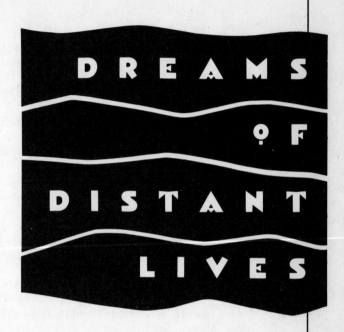

DREAMS OF DISTANT LIVES

STORIES BY
LEE K. ABBOTT

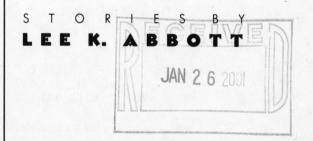

RECEIVED JAN 2 6 2001

G. P. PUTNAM'S SONS / NEW YORK

813.54
A132d

aog 4227

G. P. Putnam's Sons
Publishers Since 1838
200 Madison Avenue
New York, NY 10016

Copyright © 1989 by Lee K. Abbott
All rights reserved. This book, or parts thereof,
may not be reproduced in any form without permission.
Published simultaneously in Canada

The following stories have been published previously, some of
them in considerably different form: "The View of Me from
Mars," *Harper's;* "Here in Time and Not," *The Georgia Review;*
"Dreams of Distant Lives," *Harper's;* "Revolutionaries," *The
Atlantic;* "Once Upon a Time," *The Georgia Review;* "Why I
Live in Hanoi," *The Southern Review;* "Driving His Buick
Home," *North American Review;* "The Era of Great Numbers,"
Epoch; "1963," *The Tampa Review.*
I am indebted, as all readers should be, to Susan Kenney, whose
story "Mirrors," first published in *Epoch* and later collected in *In
Another Country,* is in part the story badly paraphrased by the
narrator of "The View of Me from Mars."

Library of Congress Cataloging-in-Publication Data

Abbott, Lee K.
Dreams of distant lives: stories /
by Lee K. Abbott.—1st American ed.
p. cm.
I. Title.
PS3551.B262D74   1989   88-28798 CIP
813' .54—dc19
ISBN 0-399-13455-7

Book design by Debbie Glasserman

Printed in the United States of America
1 2 3 4 5 6 7 8 9 10

FOR HILARY BARBER ANCKER

CONTENTS

Every shut-eye ain't asleep,
Every good-bye ain't gone.

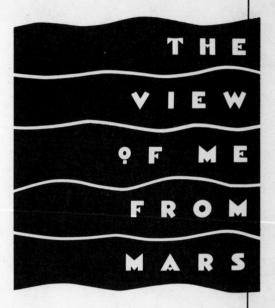

THE VIEW OF ME FROM MARS

FOR S.K.

A week before I became a father, which now seems like the long ago and far away fairy tales happen in, I read a father-child story that went straight at the surprise one truth between children and parents is. It was called "Mirrors," and had an end, to the twenty-three-year-old would-be know-it-all I was, that literally threw me back in my chair—an end, sad somehow and wise, which held that it is now and then necessary for the child, in ways mysterious with love, to forgive the parent.

In "Mirrors" the child was a girl, though it could have been a boy just as easily, whose father—a decent man, we have to believe—takes her to the sideshow tent at a one-horse and one-elephant circus in the flatlands of Iowa or Nebraska or Kansas. She's seven or eight at this time, and—as we have all begged for toys or experiences it can be, I see now, our misfortune to receive—she begs and begs to see the snake charmer

and the tattooed lady, the giant and the dwarf. He gives in, the
girl decides much later, because of his decency; or he gives in,
as my own father might say, because he's too much a milk-and-
cookies sort of fool to understand that in that smelly, ill-lit tent
is knowledge it is a parent's duty often to deny or to avoid. It
is a good moment, I tell you, this moment when they pay their
quarters and go in, one person full of pride, the other sucking
on cotton candy, the sad end of them still pages and pages
away.

   In that tent—a whole hour, I think—walking from little
stage to little stage, the girl is awestruck and puzzled and, well,
breath-taken, full of questions about where these people, these
creatures, live and what they do when they're not standing in
front of a bunch of hayseeds and would it be possible to get
a face, a tattoo, printed on her knee. "Can I touch?" she asks.
"Do they talk?" A spotlight comes on, blue and harsh, and
nearby, in a swirl of cigarette smoke and field dust, are two little
people, Mr. and Mrs. Tiny, gussied up like a commodore and
his society bride; another light snaps on, yellow this time and
ten paces away, and there stands a man—"A boy," the barker
tells us, "only eighteen and still growing!"—who's already nine
feet tall, his arms long as shovels, nothing in his face about his
own parents or what he wants to be at twenty-five. These are
clichés, my smart wife, Ellen Kay, tells me ("Sounds too artsy-
fartsy," her exact words were when I read the thing to her), but
in the story I remember, these are the exhibitions girl and man
pass by—the girl Christmas Eve impatient, the man nervous—
before they come to the main display, which is, in "Mirrors,"
a young woman, beautiful and smooth as china, who has no
arms and no legs.

   The father, complaining that he's grubby-feeling and hot,
wants to get out, but his daughter, her heart hammering in her
ears, can't move. As never before, she's conscious of her own

hands and feet, the wonders they are. She's aware of smells—
breath and oil and two-dollar cologne—and of sounds—a gasp
here, a whisper there, exclamations that have in them ache and
horror and fear. "C'mon," the father says, taking her elbow.
But onstage, businesslike as a banker, the woman—"The
Human Torso," the barker announces, "smart like the dick-
ens"—is drinking water, the glass clamped against her neck by
her shoulder; is putting on lipstick; is writing her name with
a brush between her teeth; is, Lordy, about to type—with her
chin maybe—a letter to a Spec 4 with the Army in Korea, her
boyfriend.

Outside, the midway glittering and crowded with Iowans
going crosswise, the girl, more fascinated than frightened
(though the fright is coming), asks how that was done. The
father has a Lucky Strike out now, and the narrator—seven or
eight but on the verge of learning that will stay with her until
seventy or eighty—realizes he's stalling. He's embarrassed,
maybe sick. He says "Howdy" to a deadbeat he'd never otherwise talk to. He says he's hungry, how about a hot dog, some
buttered popcorn? He's cold, he says, too cold for September.
"How?" she says again, pulling at his sleeve a little and watching his face go stiff and loose in a way that has her saying to
herself, "I am not scared. No, I am not." And then he says
what the narrator realizes will be his answer—sometimes
comic, often not—for all thereafter that astounds or baffles and
will not be known: "Mirrors, it's done with mirrors."

There's a pause here, I remember, six sentences that tell
what the weather is like and how, here and there, light bulbs
are missing and what the girl's favorite subjects are in school.
"What?" she thinks to ask, but doesn't. "It's an illusion," he
says, his voice squeaky the way it gets when he talks about
money they don't have much of. "A trick, like magic." Part of
her—the part that can say the sum of two plus two, and that

A is for Apple, B is for Boy—knows that mirrors have nothing
to do with what she's seen; another part—this the half of her
that will remember this incident forever and ever—knows that
her father, now as strange to her as the giant and the dwarf,
is lying.

His hand is working up and down, and his expression says,
as lips and eyes and cheeks will, that he's sorry, he didn't mean
for her to see that, she's so young. Something is trembling
inside her, a muscle or a bone. One-Mississippi, she says to
herself. Two-Mississippi. Over there sits a hound dog wearing
a hat and somewhere a shout is going up that says somebody
won a Kewpie doll or a stuffed monkey, and up ahead, creaking
and clanking, the Tilt-A-Whirl is full of people spinning round
and round goggle-eyed. Her father has a smile not connected
to his eyes—another lie—and his hand out to be held, and
going by them is a fat lady who lives on Jefferson Street and
a man with a limp who lives on Spruce. Her father seems too
hairy to her now, and maybe not sharp-minded enough, with
a nose too long and knobby. She tells herself what she is, which
is a good dancer and smart about which side the fork goes on
and who gets introduced first when strangers meet; and what
she is not, which is strong enough to do pull-ups and watchful
about who goes where and why. She is learning something, she
thinks. There is being good, she thinks. And there is not. There
is the truth, she thinks. And there is not.

And so, in the climax of what I read years and years ago, she
says, her hands sticky and her dress white as Hollywood daylight, "Yes, mirrors, I thought so"—words that, years and years
ago, said all I thought possible about lies and love and how
forgiveness works.

·   ·   ·

In this story, which is true and only two days old and also about forgiveness, I am the father to be read about and the child is my son, Stuart Eliot Polk, Jr. (called "Pudge" in and out of the family); he's a semifat golfer—"linksman," he insists the proper term is—and honor student who will at the end of this summer go off to college and so cease to be a citizen in the sideshow tent my big house here in El Paso now clearly is. Yes, forgiveness—particularly ironic in that, since my graduation years ago from Perkins Seminary at SMU, it has been my job to say, day after day after day, the noises that are "It will get better" and "We all make mistakes" to a thousand Methodists who aim to be themselves forgiven and sent home happy. There is no "freak" here, except the ordinary one I am, and no storybook midway, except my modern kitchen and its odd come and go.

I am an adulterer—an old-fashioned word, sure, but the only one appropriate to the ancient sin it names; and my lover—a modern word not so full of terror and guilt and judgment as another—was, until two days ago, Terri Ann Mackey, a rich, three-times-married former Zeta Tau Alpha Texas girl who might one day make headlines for the dramatic hair she has or the way she can sing Conway Twitty tunes. In every way likable and loud and free-minded, she has, in the last four years, met me anywhere and everywhere—in the Marriott and Hilton hotels, in the Cavern of Music in Juarez, even at a preachers' retreat at the Inn of the Mountain Gods near Ruidoso in southern New Mexico's piney forests. Dressed up in this or that outfit she sent away for or got on a trip to Dallas, she has, to my delight and education, pretended to be naughty as what we imagine the Swedish are or nice as Snow White; she has pretended, in a hundred rented rooms, to be everything I thought my wife was not—daring and wicked, heedless as a tyrant. Shameful to say, it seems we have always been here, in

this bright desert cowtown, now far-flung and fifty percent
ticky-tacky, drinking wine and fornicating and then hustling
home to deceive people we were wed to. Shameful to say, it
seems we have always been playing the eyes' version of footsy—
her in pink and cactus yellow in a pew in the middle of St.
Paul's, me in the pulpit sermonizing about parables and Jesus
and what welfare we owe the lost and poor and beaten down.

"Yes," my wife, Ellen Kay, would answer when I told her
I was at the Stanton Street Racquet Club playing handball
with a UTEP management professor named Red Walker. "Go
change," she'd say, herself lovely and schoolgirl trim as that
woman I'd collapsed atop a half-hour before. "I phoned," she'd
say, "Mrs. Denbo said you were out." Yes, I'd tell her. I was
in the choir room, hunting organ music that would inspire and
not be hokey; I was in the library, looking up what the Puritan
Mathers had written about witchcraft and gobbledygook we
are better off without; I was taking a drive in my Volvo, the
better to clear my head so I could get to the drafting of a
speech for the Rotarians, or the LULAC Club of Ysleta, or the
Downtown Optimists. "You work too hard," she'd say, "let's
go to Acapulco this year." And I'd head to my big bedroom,
the men I am, the public one amazed by his private self—the
first absolutely in love with a blonde continental-history major
he'd courted at the University of Texas in 1967; the second still
frazzled by what, in the afternoon, is made from deceit and
bednoise and indecency. And until two days ago, it was possible
to believe that I knew which was which, what what.

"Where were you?" Ellen Kay said, making (though too
violently, I think now) the tuna casserole I like enough to eat
twice a year. "I called everywhere," she said. "It was as if you
didn't exist." Upset, her hair spilling out of the French roll she
prefers, she said more, two or three paragraphs whose theme
was my peculiar behavior and the sly way I had lately and what

time I was supposed to be somewhere and was not; and suddenly, taking note of the thump-thump my heart made and
how one cloud in the east looked like a bell, I stood at the sink,
steadily drinking glass after glass of water, trying to put some
miles between me and her suspicions. Terri Ann Mackey Cruz
Robinson Cross was all over me, my hands and my thighs and
my face; and, a giant step away, my wife was asking where I'd
been. "You were going to call," Ellen Kay said. "You had an
appointment, a meeting." I had one thought, which was about
the bricked-up middle of me, and another, which was about
how like TV this situation was. "I talked to Bill Watson at the
bank," she said. "He hasn't seen you for a week, ten days. I
called—" And her wayward husband had a moment then,
familiar to all cheaters and sorry folks, when he thought he'd
tell the truth; a moment, before fear hit him and he got a 3-D
vision of the cheap world he'd have to live in, when he thought
to make plain the creature he was and the no-account stage he
stood upon.

"I was at the golf course," I said, "watching Pudge. They
have a match tomorrow." The oven was closed, the refrigerator
opened. "Which course?" she said. Forks and knives had been
brought out, made a pile of. "Coronado Hills," I said. "Pudge
is hitting the ball pretty good." She went past me a dozen
times, carrying the plates and the bread and the fruit bowl, and
I tried to meet her eyes and so not give away the corrupt inside
of me. I thought of several Latin words—*bellum* and *verus* and
fatum—and the Highland Park classroom I learned them in.
"All right," she said, though by the dark notes in her voice it
was clear she was going to ask Pudge if he'd seen me there, by
the green I'd claimed to have stood next to, applauding the
expert wedge shot I'd seen with my very own eyes.

As in the former story of illusions and the mess they make
crashing down, there is a pause here, one of two; and you are

to imagine now how herky-jerky time moved in our house when
Pudge drove up and came in and said howdy and washed his
hands as he'd been a million times told. You are to imagine,
too, the dinner we picked at and our small talk about school
and American government and what money does. While time
went up and down, I thought about Pudge the way evil comic-
book Martians are said to think about us: I was curious to know
how I'd be affected by what, in a minute or an hour, would
come from the mouth of an earthling who, so far as I knew,
had never looked much beyond himself to see the insignificant
dust ball he stood upon. I saw him as his own girlfriend, Traci
Dixon, must: polite, fussy as a nun, soft-spoken about everything except golf and how it is, truly, a full-fledged sport.

Part of me—that eye and ear which would make an excellent
witness at an auto wreck or similar calamity—flew up to one
high corner of the room, like a ghost or an angel, and wondered
what could be said about these three people who sat there and
there and there. They were Democrats who, in a blue moon,
liked what Reagan did; they had Allstate insurance and bank
books and stacks of paper that said where they were in the
world and what business they conducted with it; they played
Scrabble and Clue and chose to watch the news Dan Rather
read. The wife, who once upon a time could run fast enough
to be useful in flag football, now used all her energy to keep
mostly white-collar rednecks from using the words "nigger"
and "spic" in her company; the son, who had once wanted to
be an astronaut or a Houston brain surgeon, now aimed to be
the only Ph.D. in computer science to win the Masters at
Augusta, Georgia; and the father—well, what was there to say
about a supposedly learned man for whom the spitting image
of God, Who was up and yonder and everywhere, was his own
father, a bent-over and gin-soaked cattle rancher in Midland,
Texas? I hovered in that corner, distant and disinterested, and

then Ellen Kay spoke to Pudge, and I came rushing back, dumb and helpless as anything human that falls from a great height.

"Daddy says you had a good round this afternoon," Ellen Kay began. "You had an especially nice wedge shot, he says." She was being sneaky, which my own sneaky self admired; and Pudge quit the work his chewing was, a little confusion in his round, smart face. He was processing, that machine between his ears crunching data that in no way could ever be, and for the fifteen seconds we made eye contact I wanted him to put aside reason and logic and algebra and see me with his guts and heart. On his lip he had a crumb that, if you didn't tell him, would stay until kingdom come; I wanted him to stop blinking and wrinkling his forehead like a first-year theater student. The air was heavy in that room, the light coming from eight directions at once, and I wanted to remind him of our trip last January to the Phoenix Open and that too-scholarly talk we'd had about the often mixed-up relations between men and women. I had a picture of me throwing a ball to him, and of him catching it. I had a picture of him learning to drive a stick shift, and of him so carefully mowing our lawn. Oddly, I thought about fishing, which I hate, and bowling, which I am silly at, and then Ellen Kay, putting detergent in the dishwasher, asked him again about events that never happened, and I took a deep breath I expected to hold until the horror stopped.

Here is that second pause I spoke of—that moment, before time lurches forward again, when the eye needs to look elsewhere to see what is ruined, what not. Pudge now knew I was lying. His eyes went here and there, to the clock above my shoulder, to his mother's overwatered geranium on the windowsill, to his mostly empty plate. He was learning something about me—and about himself too. Like his made-up counterpart in "Mirrors," he was seeing that I, his father, was afraid and weak and damaged; and like the invented daddy in that story I read, a daddy whose interior life we were not permitted to see, I wanted my own child, however numbed or shocked, to forgive me for the tilt the world now stood at, to say I was not responsible for the sad magic trick our common back-and-forth really is. "Tell her," I said. I had in mind a story he could confirm—the Coke we shared in the clubhouse, a corny joke that was heard, and the help I tried to be with his short game—a story that had nowhere in it, two days ago, a father cold and alone and small.

THE
HAPPY
PARTS

Too soon after my divorce—itself mainly an hour of ink and paper, plus several Latin tongue twisters from a judge named J. Andrew Felter—I'm standing in the foyer of Helen's house in Shaker Heights. Helen is Helen Riddick, one lover of mine and another reason I'm single now, and her house is a French-style pile of bricks big enough, I swear, for two zip codes—a place with five fireplaces, each of which I, naked and drunk, have lit, sat beside or watched burn all damn out.

"Oh, Ricky, Ricky, Ricky," she's saying, patting my arm and wagging her head like the mother she twice over is. "You must feel terrible. Rotten. Here, go in there and just be comfortable."

Her living room is part *Town & Country,* part Ponderosa, and I should feel heartened, but don't, to sit again on furniture I go back to childhood with.

"I'm fine," I tell her. "I'm not a worrier."

With the exception of fifteen years, when she was at Colorado College and then in Los Angeles, where she met Jack, her husband, we've known each other more or less continuously—since high school in Las Cruces, New Mexico, where we were Bulldogs together and careless youngsters from that desert's ruling class. She was Helen Tibbets then, blonde as a starlet and the owner of a Mustang V-8 convertible, and I was William Richard Mackey, citizen of the country club and entirely too slack-witted to imagine the generally adequate pediatrician I've become.

"Drink something," she hollers from down the hall. Pantry, maybe. "Jack won't miss it."

Jack is John Mather Riddick, a senior partner with Ridley, Wallace (America's, so they say, second-largest law firm) and, from my view, a white-bread-and-mayonnaise sort of guy it now makes no sense to have cuckolded. He used to be a Malibu surfer, a bona fide beach boy, and afternoons, standing shoulder to shoulder with him on the concrete collar of his pool, I've seen him grow misty-eyed over the cheerful lights his blue water makes. Where he is now is Mexico City. "Hiding dollars," his exact phrase was. "I feel like the frigging Easter Bunny."

Now Helen is walking out of the dining room. A tape has come on, aggressively up-tempo rock 'n' roll with serious wah-wah, plus an armylike chorus of clearly angry women. "I like to stay current," she's said a million times. "It's my downfall."

"Where are the girls?" I ask.

She makes a wave, too much wrist, by which, if she were the Amazing Kreskin or another whose hocus-pocus I delight in, half the house could have vanished. "At the Shelbys'," she says. "A sleep-over. Then the skating club tomorrow. Little Miss Fixit, that's me."

I pour a second drink, Dewar's, and see if anything's going on outdoors besides snow.

"You're a free man now," Helen says. And next a word that may, or may not, have genuine mirth in it: "Congratulations."

Winter is four feet deep, and it is possible to conceive of February in terms of years.

"Where's Elaine?" she's asking.

Home, I guess. I'm supposed to drop by later, pick up some stuff. Papers, I think. Odds and ends I overlooked when I moved into the Alcazar Hotel in the Heights last April.

"I like her," Helen informs me. "This'll bring us closer, her and me. She's a Libra, isn't she?"

"Aquarius," I say. "Air sign."

Helen gives me the look she uses for the maid. "Even better."

For the next hour, we gab—she more than I—and two more tapes go by. I hear a song called "Important Moments in the History of Russia" and watch my foot doing a tap-tap-tap I find myself losing when the screaming starts. I tell Helen about my lawyer, Ron Mundy, the beer I had with him and the two lines of coke that were his idea of a present. He kept saying "Whoopee" the whole hour, indicating where I was to sign, doing the ABCs of my new status, forms flying across his desk like the poker cards used in Wonderland. At the end of it—the real end, not the fake end, when he told me to buck the hell up, look on the bright side, all that rah-rah junk—he marched around his desk, hoisted me to my feet to see how busy downtown looked from forty stories up.

"I got a law degree from Mars," he said. "I know squat. It's the brunettes outside who do the typing, they know the lingo. This is the diddly I do, Ricky: I smile, speak real fast, and cash appears for my pastimes. I have to find a new trade."

At five-sixteen, so the fat guy on Channel 8 says, the sun sets, and I check outdoors to see if he's right.

"Let's call some people," I say.

Helen has her second outfit on, a skirt-shirt affair that suggests "cocktails" and "tropics." She still has the legs of a cheerleader, in particular smooth hamstrings that should be ooohhhed over by the grown-ups who could be here in, as is said in my corner of the world, two shakes of a lamb's tail.

"Not a good idea," she suggests. "You're grieving, remember? You just got divorced, remember? Your life is crumbling, in disarray, et cetera."

Across the boulevard, four lanes of road with a shrub-covered median, now almost another country, downstairs lights have switched on, and I am struck by a notion that once upon a time I might've told Elaine about.

"You're kidding," Helen says. "Jesus H. Christ, Ricky. Get real."

No, I tell her. I hike over, I make introductions, I invite. *Uno, dos, tres*—that's how the drill works.

"Be my guest," Helen says, and seconds later I'm in this *Esquire-*magazine topcoat I own, halfway down Helen's sidewalk. I am up to my knees in snow, and I am speaking to my nearly frozen feet the way it is sometimes necessary to address things—the lawn mower, for example, the can opener—that just aren't working they way they ought. *"Uno,"* I'm saying. *"Dos."* I consider the sky, I consider the wind, and there is a moment, before I understand it is not Helen I want to sleep with tonight, when I think to bag it, this trip across the street, and go back indoors where it is warm and dry and rich.

Then I hear it, this voice I also want to tell about.

"Hi, I'm Monique," it's saying, a woman's. "And I have two friends that are just dying to meet you—"

I graduated cum laude from the University of New Mexico. I have an M.D. from Washington University in St. Louis. I have a practice on Green Road at Chagrin, one damaged knee and a Volvo wagon in need of a ring job: I absolutely do not hear voices.

"Bonjour, je m'appelle Monique." The voice has a lot of teenager in it, but little conviction. "I know what you want, I—"

It's like one of those 976 numbers, and I'm hunting around for the joke—maybe Helen hollering from a window above me. I look, as is said, high and low. At last, I assume it's the booze, or a neighbor kid with a Mr. Microphone and a prankster's sense of humor. Maybe the outdoor speakers all the neighbors seem to have around their decks or swimming pools. Something goofy. A too-loud TV, maybe. Modern TV and the way the wind blows.

"I'm from Nice," the voice says before it clicks off. *"Mes amies* are, uh, Rachel and Daphne. We—"

When I reach the curb, I'm thinking about St. Bart's, the island I visited with Elaine summer before last. Down the road, a dozen houses away, a car is coming forward slowly, and I'm remembering how my wife, my ex, looks in wet bathing clothes, that "Ouch" she squeals when the surf's too cold. Then the car's next to me, beyond and stopped.

"Pete Parker," I say.

The car's a VW Jetta, well dinged, and immediately it backs up to prove me right.

"Hey, partner," I hear. A window has rolled down and leaning toward the passenger side and grinning is the face of a man who—was it three years ago?—stood in my living room to holler all that was known about Nicaragua and the Vermont sweetheart he had down there named Lorraine. Or Lurline. A Catholic lay worker with *l*s and Karl Marx's appreciation of good and bad.

"Need a lift?" he wonders.

You betcha, I say, and climb in.

"Where to?"

His is the voice of Dan-Dee potato chips. And Kellogg's Corn Flakes. And St. Luke's Impotence Center. Pip's Instant Printing. He does commercials—the talent, he's called—mostly out of Pittsburgh and Chicago. He has a spot on now—that's another word, "spot"—half a minute, about this season's men's suits and where to buy them cheap.

"Listen," I tell him, "this is crazy, I'm only going across the street."

The plows have thrown huge snowbanks on the median and I have an unflattering vision of myself shouting "Mush, mush" in the middle of it.

"No problem," Pete says. Pete Parker.

So off we start to the turnaround, eight hundred yards to go twenty.

"Got a date?" I say.

"It's the cologne, isn't it?" he says. "I get carried away. Lu Ann used to claim I was afraid of my own body, the smell."

Wrong, I tell him. It's the fancy tie, the sportcoat. The whatever.

"I overcompensate," he's saying. "Bad habit. It's a kid thing, very infantile. When I get nervous, the whole image falls apart."

We reach the crossover, make the turn, and damned if it hasn't stopped snowing. I wonder how the streets are where I used to live, about ten blocks farther on. I like snow, I'm thinking. I really do.

"This it?" Pete asks.

We're stopped opposite my car, and several things about Helen's house yonder—the shut curtains, the partly open storm door—don't appear even a little bit encouraging.

"I'm really sorry about you and Elaine," Pete's saying.

It happens, I tell him. You got to be brave. Buck the hell up.

"Ain't that the truth," he says, but another sentence has occurred to him before he can let my door close. "It's the inner life. My first wife, the one after college, claimed I had the psychology of a timber wolf. You get to be crazy now, I guess. Take it from me. This a period nobody can hold against you."

So we've said *adiós* and he's down the street, turning carefully, and going again the way we went. Pete Parker. The voice of Glenbeigh Hospital. He waves as he passes, a snappy gesture with some U.S. Army in it, and I haul myself, plus my inner life, toward the door I aimed for many minutes ago.

I'm not bitter, I tell myself. Actually, I have fifty thoughts—about the age I am, which is forty-one, and how the office will be tomorrow, and how, for a baby doctor, I don't like children much—all of which seem as far off from me as heaven, and all of which, big and small, I put right out of mind when I get to the door and punch the bell.

"Hold your horses," I hear, a man, so I turn, and across the way, in an upstairs window, stands Helen. Throwing me the finger the way she did when we were kids.

This time she's nude.

. . . .

The guy who answers the door goes about six-five, 240 maybe, a textbook mesomorph, and eyeballs me like I'm from Tibet or somewhere. Besides his parka, he's wearing mittens and a fur hat that might look neat on any head in Alaska.

"Where's your gear?" he says. "Your truck. The tools."

I shrug, endeavor to appear agreeable.

"Let me guess," he begins. "You're not from Divita's, the heating people."

I'm disappointed to say no—my eager-beaver's chronic need
to please, I guess—but he's already moving, telling me to come
in, close the door. "Colder than a witch's tit," he says. "Furnace went bust." The place is a warehouse of boxes and crates
and the other freebies Allied gives you; it's hard to tell whether
there's been a recent moving in or about to be a moving out.
"Find a place," he's saying. "Try the kitchen. I'm on the
phone."

Piled against one wall in the dining room (which has two
chandeliers and enough hardwood for a bowling alley), is furniture—chairs, an oak end table, an ottoman, a love seat from
one of the French Louises, brass floor lamps—that looks like
whatever the poor man's version of Holiday Inn is. "Kitchen,"
I remind myself, having two doors to pick between.

I don't know it yet, but this guy—Mike, his name turns
out—is a sports and entertainment agent with the McCormack
group downtown, the outfit that owns Arnold Palmer and every
third professional athlete in North America. So when I open
a door and discover, sitting around a table, three beautiful
women in more or less show biz evening wear, I have no idea
that they're clients—"Singers," he'll tell me, "like the Go-
Go's, or Bananarama"; I just think they're outdamnstanding
and awfully much like the women it has been my mistake to
fall in and out of love with too often in the eleven years I was
married.

"You the man?" The one asking has that asymmetrical
hairdo said to be fashionable in New York, plus shiny teeth that
bring up one or two unwelcome thoughts in me.

"Afraid not," I answer.

The oven is open, the gas burners going full blast, and for
an instant I am warmed and overwhelmed by the smell of
them, their very painted toenails and the hi-de-ho statements
their outfits are—*three friends dying to meet you.* They're

playing a card game that involves slapping the table, laughter and gulping from Cuervo bottles.

"What's the story with Mike?"

"Phone," I say, and we regard each other as if there might be more to know. She could be twenty-two, or forty. "How 'bout a drink?"

Help yourself, I'm told. In the cupboard. While I'm doing my looking, I'm entertained by what these women know about a man named Whitey. He's a Nazi, I hear. A running wound. A classic passive-aggressive. Whitey the weasel. Whitey, real name Adelbert. What a pimple.

"What's Mike drinking?"

They all give me who-are-you looks, so I grab a bottle of black-label Jack Daniel's, two glasses, and bid adieu.

"Whitey," one mutters to the cards she's dealt. "What a weeb."

A hand smacks the table, hard, and the woman nearest the door, the redhead with the thousand-dollar posture, says, "Banzai, Loretta. Drink up."

In the living room, box-filled too and cluttered with magazines like *Creem* and *Spin* and *PAC-10 Gridiron Digest*, Mike is having a war with the phone. I pour him three fingers of bourbon—that's how we expressed it in my dad's house, fingers—which he accepts with a nod and an ugly gesture at the mouthpiece. "That's a can-do, baby," he's saying. "I am receiving you in stereo." His face says *No way, José,* but his voice remains four kinds of sympathy. "Baby, I understand. They're mutants, cretins. But you're the dingdong on this one, sweetheart. A–number one, baby." Mike points me to a chair that requires only a minute to clear off. It was covered with Z-fold paper, what looked like every fraction in the universe.

"Cheers," I say, content to be here. He has a fire going, with easily a week's worth of *Miami Herald*s, and I'm trying to figure out a way to apologize for the drip marks I've left on the way I've come.

"Deep breaths, baby," he's saying. "Calm down. It's a glitch, a blip—not worth the uproar. We rip their arms off, baby. Do things with the stumps." He takes a drink, buries the phone against his parka. "I hate this bitch," he tells me. "Day in, day out, it's yabba-yabba. It's blah-blah-blah. I want my shrink to crack her head, see if there's a rat in there or what." His conversation is mostly "baby-this" and "baby-that," and I'm thinking it's his girlfriend. His wife.

"That's a killer line, baby," he says. "Super. Write that sucker down, will you?"

Who knows, maybe it's his daughter. His mother. Then there are some kissing noises, the phone's hung up, and I've come to the conclusion that I'm sixty percent sober, not sixty percent hammered. In the last three days I've eaten twice, I think. Breakfast Tuesday at Norton's. Half a chicken salad lunch yesterday. Nothing since Ron Mundy informed me he was from Mars.

"Mike," he says.

I like the guy's smile, which is crooked and involves everything but his hair.

"Jack," I tell him. "Across the street." I'm feeling sporty, the way I was when, at least a century ago, I asked a former Zeta Tau Alpha named Elaine to be my wife. Maybe, I ask Mike, he's met her already.

"Can't say."

Monique, I tell him. Tall woman. Looks like a jazz dancer.

"Haven't met anybody, pal." He's poking at the fireplace, a guy who knows his way around home fires. "I live in airports, man. Stapleton, D/FW, O'Hare. I know just about every concierge in every Hyatt in the States."

I hear about his business then, the acts he represents, the

deals he does. He hails from Jackson, Mississippi, played football at Tulane, nose tackle; sixth-round draft choice of Atlanta,
made the cut; a few years down the line, he's the player rep
for the Falcons, learning the dollars-and-cents half of sports.
"Next," he says, "it's bingo-bango and here I am, middle
middle-age, being smart for Mötley Crüe and the like. O. J.
Simpson." Mike handles shelters, real estate, talks the talk. He
shakes the hands, pats the backs, eats a shitload of carryout.
"Take Bliss, for instance."

I have a bourbon I can't remember drinking, and a fierce
desire to have more. I like it here. I really do.

"The girls," Mike's saying. "In the kitchen."

Right, I nod. Whitey the weasel.

"I found them in Minneapolis," he says. "We signed with
CBS last week." They're from Ripon College, he says. Philosophy majors. Or continental studies. Hell, he doesn't know what
point they're making. Songs like "Blow Your Cool." And
"More Facts About Life." One girl—Loretta, he believes—
worked for EDS, Ross Perot's thing in Dallas, two summers
ago. They're communists, he thinks. Trotskyites. *People* magazine ought to eat them up. They're like nuns who strip.

Another stack of papers—*The Houston Post*, this time—
goes on the fire, and it's somebody's turn to talk about me.

"Doctor," I announce.

He has a trick with his head and lineman's eyebrows that
implies I'm putting him on, so, because it's true, I get loud. It's
partly the liquor.

"No kidding," I say, but it comes out with an extra *d*. I have
a million words: colic, edema, ringworm, the Asian flu every
winter, projectile vomit. I'm from the Southwest, I say, a
monster cattle ranch on the mesa toward Deming. I have a
sister who works for United Airlines, a string-bean brother-in-
law in Denver, three nephews who are the stars of the Billy

Kidd ski school in Vail. I'm a Democrat, I think. Make sixty, sixty-five K a year. Used to smoke.

"I know facts about kids that'd make you sick," I say.

Mike's looking at me kooky, so I mention women, one of whom is skinny and tough-minded as a judge, Elaine, but it's after our fourth Black Jack and I'm thinking I have the biographical data of a lizard. From the kitchen you can hear shouting about—what?—Kant perhaps, and how the Germans are teaching these days.

"I don't believe he's coming," Mike says. "Divita."

I'm in complete agreement. "The heater guy."

We've reached a dead stop, Mike and I, and I realize it's the minute to pull my coat on, leave.

"Sorry," he says. He has more calls to make, *beaucoup* calls. A midget comedian in Hawaii, a magician in Tokyo. They need his input. Plus he has to arrange for a limo to pick up the girls; they've rooms at the Bond Court, no sense wasting money.

"Absolutely," I say, though it comes out with too much spit.

A gentleman, he escorts me to the door, but when he tells me to take care, nice meeting me, because half of me is dreading where I must go next, I tell him who I really am. William Richard Mackey. Ricky, Ricky, Ricky. My insides are going flip-flop, I can't get my gloves on, and he's saying no matter, no sweat, he didn't figure we were buddies yet.

"You come back sometime," he says. "We'll start over."

The door opens, winter has not disappeared, and two steps later I'm wondering who the hell baby is.

Baby-this and baby-that.

·   ·   ·

Now this is definitely one happy part.

Helen's house is closed down, dark. Virtually nailed shut.

And I'm thinking about feelings, the crossways I once was. I used to be a chatterbox, real mouthy; these days I'm a yup-nope guy, Gary Cooper without the stiff spine. I used to read—novels, *The Plain Dealer,* you name it. Had a subscription to *Mother Jones,* wrote letters of protest to Dow Chemical and IBM. Nowadays even a paragraph tuckers me out. I've gone into what TV says the world is, which is clamorous and colorful and simple. I used to like dancing—the cha-cha, the rhumba, the tango I learned in Cotillion—the classy left-and-right that can be done upright with a woman in your arms. Mostly, however, I just have shoot-'em-up dreams of the Wild West, the long-limbed galoot my sleepworld urges me to be.

My house, my ex-house, is dark too; but out of habit, what my muscles and brain did for the nearly five years Elaine and I lived there together, I park in the garage, yank the door down. The drive's been plowed, so there's no evidence I've been anywhere near the place. Elaine's Toyota is here, cleaner than I remember, and one reason I get the key from its hiding place under a paint can next to the firewood: the combination of the silence and how the snow looks tells me she's not home, makes me ignore by the back door the boxes I am supposed to tote off.

Inside I say hello—honest Injun—to the furniture I recognize. I see myself on the sofa, settled like a priest. I see Elaine as the nurse I courted, whose white outfits were color and state of mind both. I see again the outrageous way she drives, which is with her legs spread and with one careless hand, and for twenty seconds—time that has weight and movement and sound—I am in love again. I hear the cat she bought at the pound—Mr. Bee is his name—and wonder where he is, what we'll make of each other when we meet.

"A drink," I say. "One for the road."

I think X, I think Y, and just when I'm thinking about the fist Elaine clobbered me with one Christmas, a car pulls in the drive, a Jetta, and I am reminded how wonderful the world largely is.

"Pete Parker," I say. His cologne. His inner life.

I've had one fistfight in my life. In junior high, with Philip Trafton. It was about his cello that I was supposed to have knocked over during orchestra rehearsal. This fight happened on the playground. "Go on," he said. "Be a tough guy." He let me smack him maybe six times, then he picked up his instrument, walked off limping, and I went to the doctor to get an X ray for my wrist. Which is the story I'm telling myself as I go from my picture window to my former bedroom upstairs, and why I find myself so composed, sitting on the foot of the bed, when Elaine Jansen Mackey comes in the side door with a man who is the urgent voice of Ray Miller Buick-Isuzu.

They are laughing, then they are not. The TV has gone on, *Nightline,* and I can almost puzzle out what Ted Koppel is telling us about debt and, ironically, what it costs. I hear Pete say "Howdy Doody" and a giggle from Elaine that I take to be affirmative; then—by the way the air is and how the walls move—I know they are kissing. She is kissing, well, backward—her head cocked left, not right, in a way that always left me unable to hold her—and I hope for Pete Parker's sake that he doesn't open his eyes to discover that she is, as she often was with me, staring at him, her big eyes not part of the moment her lips are.

"Yes," I'm whispering. "You betcha."

The bed is soft, no wind is to be heard, and, before I lay me down, I know, just as I know my own name, who the hell baby is.

I really do.

HERE
IN
TIME
AND NOT

The times I told this story of first love while it was going on, I screwed it up—its parts mismated, its time haywire as that in nightmares, or its people like made-up creatures from storybooks and not the flesh and type O blood they are in my household. I got it wrong because I did not, could not, see my family—my older son, Buddy (about whom this mostly is), my wife, Darlene, and my younger son, Craig John—as my friend Fudge Walker says is right, which has to do with a pal's sympathy and (so he says) a Martian's disinterest.

Fudge Walker, who is our golf pro and affects a sportsman's view of human activity, claims love is itself a game, by which he means that it involves risk and rewards and common happenstance; but he's on his third wife now and tries damn hard to look at the funny side of what can be won and lost in love. My in-laws, who heard Buddy's story last Xmas when we visited their ranch in Roswell, say love is a fine thing ("Hunky-

dory," my jolly father-in-law's words were; "jim dandy") and
very useful, which is wisdom you evidently achieve after thirty-
plus years you have no desire to look back on too suspiciously.
My wife, whose own first love was a 216-pound high schooler
named Wicks, doesn't say much on the subject, but there are
times—when we are watching something drippy on TV or
when she is tired and loose-minded from cocktails—that I
suspect she is thinking of a letter-club president more gentle
than we expect all-district outside linebackers to be.

My own view—the one I arrived at joylessly in my Buick on
Interstate 25 outside of Socorro, about 120 miles north of the
town of Hatch, where we live in New Mexico—is that first love
has only a little to do with what Hallmark rhymes about, or how
our glands make us hop, or what is invented to entertain the
wishful thinkers we now and then are. The point of first love
is to hurt us, deeply and permanently.

My son knows this now. I saw the truth of it in Buddy's face
and arms and blue eyes one night last week after he'd broken
up with his girlfriend.

"It will get better," I said, which was one overused sentence
that occurred to me. I told him, yes, that he'd laugh about this
one day, that he'd survive—all the lines that are standard and
important, parent to child.

"I don't want to talk about it," he said.

We were at my kitchen table, me reading the *Sun News* to
find out how dumb some Americans had been that day, and
him flipping through the tenth-grade mathematics he's supposed to be sharp enough to master. Polynomials were not on
his mind, I could tell. Rather, he was wrought up with bitter-
ness and grief, his brain collapsed sideways and not in any way
ready for the silly xs and ys numbers sometimes are.

"It hurts like hell," he said finally. "Is that what you want
to hear?"

. . .

Her name is Stacy and she became Buddy's girlfriend during the spring last year, when he was an entirely adequate third baseman for the Alameda Junior High School Falcons. Though nothing like my own first love—Leonna Allen, now a registered nurse who lives in Lubbock, Texas—Stacy was as perfect and sure of herself as every first love appears to be; and, as I have told Buddy, he went for her as I, in eleventh-grade history, went for Leonna Allen—which, in the moon-June-swoon poetry I learned, is described as tumbling and falling and being, well, rent with life. Something opens up in you, I have decided. A vessel, or a cavity, or an organ, and for a while thereafter you are a rocking-chair philosopher who sees significance in all the objects and rigmarole and ideas you bump into day by day by day. Sofas have meaning, as do what is eaten by the two of you and how the weather whirls. Everything is secret, and you are made so strong—by words and touch and smell—that you wonder how you managed to live without it.

That's what Leonna Allen did to me. Tall (Stacy is medium) and thin (Stacy is thicker through the shoulders) and quiet (Stacy is, like me, a blabbermouth), Leonna sat behind me in Mrs. Sutherland's class, and one day she tapped me on the back to ask me to name again the British kings and queens whose order we'd studied; and suddenly—there is no other word that recollects the thunderclap love is—I was absolutely smitten. My past (which had my father and his heart attacks, and my mother and her alcoholism) vanished completely; and my future (which has come to have property and wealth) seemed impossible. I had only what Darlene calls an eternal moment: electric and weird, physical as a fistfight.

In the old story this is, Leonna Allen did not love me back. She loved Rodney Tate, a senior with a car and pocket money and, from my view, nothing remotely intellectual on his mind.

"What happened to him?" Buddy asked at a basketball game.

Rodney Tate had gone to Vietnam, I thought.

"He died, right?"

(No, I was able to answer the other day, Rodney Tate did not die, for he resides now in Houston and is himself married to a woman with a cheery telephone voice and manners enough to humor someone like me pestering about the past.)

"Did you hate him?" Buddy asked.

As is not the case now, when it is possible, even healthy, to loathe the cheaters who govern and disappoint us or the bad guys who maim and murder and violate the rule of innocence we ought to live by, I hated no one. Or I hated—which is the bottom half of passion, I think—only me, particularly that me who traipsed after Leonna Allen like a scrawny, milky-eyed hound dog looking for food. I drove by her home when I could, night and day; or I'd beg my friends Jay Bullard and Mark Runyan to drive me by so I could see which lights were hers and if, from the signs a house can give, she would ever love me. I even gave her my letter sweater with the big red-and-blue H I earned for being a good-humored duffer on a golf team made up of bookworms and two kids who were cut from the swim club.

"I can't do this, Archie," she said. "You're sweet to ask, but it wouldn't be right. I have a boyfriend."

I had lugged it to school in a fancy box, and it had no meaning if she did not wear it.

"Honest, I understand," I told her. "What about when the weather gets cold?"

She accepted it, I think now, because she appreciated, if not the sweater itself, certainly the feeling it stood for. She respected it as I, and the folks I intend to line up behind in the hereafter, respect the symbols that are hereabouts important: wedding bands, the starchy collar the Reverend Ellis wears, the badge my old buddy George Toomer has for being sheriff—all the things smart-asses in the big world giggle at and have figured out how to make money from.

Buddy had symbols, too. Last year, he gave record albums to Stacy—U2 and Tears for Fears and Hoodoo Gurus, whose lyrics talked about the place he lived in and were themselves the sentences he felt. On her birthday in September, he gave her a Longines watch, whose purchase he'd mowed lawns and caddied for. It told only time—no special features like dates or what hour it is in Moscow—but it stood for something: for why he used Jade East cologne and why he kept his room more picked up than usual and why he wouldn't let anyone but his mother trim his hair. It wasn't sentimentality, which is what dummies say emotion is; it was sentiment, which is the opening and closing of you and the marvel that anything about you—your hands or sloppy legs—works and maybe even gets better.

The day after he bought the watch, I tried to discuss this observation with him while we fixed a window in the garage. For five minutes I went on with the oooo-la-la and dizziness these feelings were. "Ain't it grand?" I asked. "Don't you feel like a million bucks?"

Buddy gave me a look that came from the bottom of him: "C'mon, Dad, leave me alone." With his hair flopped over one eye and five pimples on his cheeks, he looked too young for the adventure he was on.

"I can tell you what to watch for," I said.

He shook his head. "Maybe later, okay? Not now."

So the window was repaired and the watch delivered, and I got to observe—as maybe Rodney Tate had observed me—and wait.

Love turns you into a son of a bitch. What I did not see in me years ago, but what became clear in the example that was my son, is that love—the weight and density it is, even the private lingo it has—shifts and twists the world away: time becomes wretched, topsy-turvy and wrong; nothing about you fits; even our gizmos—the stove, the car, the TV—fail to do what they should. You are exiled and cross-hearted, hiking uphill when everyone else you see is running down. My own father, who is dead and probably golfing in the dry purgatory he believed in, said he came close one time to beating the holy stuffings out of me in the days first love made me brutish and proud.

"For your own good," my father said after this incident ended. "You'll thank me one day."

In history, this happened two weeks after Kennedy was killed. I was sixteen, my father sixty, and on the Saturday I am concerned with we were alone in our living room (the one, fittingly, I now own and into which my son goes only to pout in the darkness). My father was practicing his putting stroke, sending ball after ball across the carpet toward a water glass he'd put in the dining room. "It's Red Mather on the eighteenth green," he was saying, whispering as if there were ten million in TV-land to hear him. "This is for the Masters and lasting goddamn fame." He had a match in an hour and was dressed in a fashion a certain lovestruck youngster had no tolerance for: white Nutonic spikes, slacks the green that garbage trucks come in, a yellow shirt I have dreamed about once or twice.

"The crowd is hushed," my father was saying. "You can hear a you-know-what drop, you know?"

For too long he stood over his putts, serious as a surgeon, and for too long I listened to one click after another. I was waiting for Leonna to call; we'd planned to drive to the new mall in Las Cruces thirty miles away, and I wanted to be with her, not in my living room watching my daddy pretend he was Orville "Sarge" Moody (just as, in more recent times, Buddy has wanted to be with Stacy and not on the couch listening to his own father pretend to be wise like "Dear Abby").

I could hear everything that day (hearing being only one sense love sharpens): Ugg Mackey's collie dog yapping, a man on KOBE radio saying who Oswald was, my own heart going clomp-*clomp*. I had no place to put my hands, or my feet. I could not read the *Life* magazine in my lap, or make real its wild full-page pictures. Yes, I checked the phone—once, twice, three times—and dashed outside to look up the street for the signals nature owes those in love. But I could see only flaws: tarnished silver, a crack in the marble coffee table, a portrait of us that made us look crooked and a little bit like criminals.

"I've had just about enough of you," my daddy said at last.

This could have been the man in the moon yammering, and I felt a need to be silent and wide-eyed.

"C'mere," he said. "Sit your butt down."

He had the mayhem-filled face of the welterweight he'd been at Dartmouth College a million years ago, so I did as ordered.

"When are you going to grow up?"

Those were his words—which were enough like mine, that time Buddy and I were fixing the window, to be scary—but they blew by me that day as dumb as the wind. I was concentrating, instead, on the thwack-thwack his putter made in his hand, and how he seemed to be taking up most of the light in the universe.

"This won't do," my daddy was saying. "This is how a stray dog behaves. Next you'll be outdoors bawling."

I regarded him the way a human regards a bird that can

chatter a paragraph or two of English. There was a defense I
tried to make—a justifying of my ups and downs, a speech that
accounted for the special chemicals and hopes running in
me—but my father wasn't hearing any of it. The lawyer in him
was going, wearing a path back and forth in front of me. There
was stuff I needed to know, he was saying. The mechanics of
boy and girl: pubic hair and puberty, and how to bait your hook
(which was his semi-wise metaphor for the catching and keeping of love). Yelling and pacing, he drew me pictures of the
uproar I stood in. "It is war," he said. "It is commerce," he
said. And more: hubbub and sweet talk and slack-wittedness
and shilly-shally that topples you away from goodness.

He informed me of the running-down love was, the hollow
clank you notice when it one day stops. It was a building up,
he said, and a tearing down. Love, the thing he was talking
about and the way he was talking about it, was only jibber-
jabber, a language we either learn or shut our goddamn mouths
about.

"You understand?" he said.

His face was red, his putter in the air like a war club, and
my head went yes for one solid minute, I swear.

"Good," he said, and in the end of a special scene in my life,
my father brought that putter down, yanked it out of the air
in a fury, and whacked off a corner of our marble table the size
of an emperor's dinner dish.

"Now *that*," he began, giving me the wink he was famous
for, "is something real to fret about."

. . . .

For the three months after Buddy fell in love, instead of butt-
ing in and checking up, I kept watch over the steady rise and
fall of my here and now. I pushed my memories aside, as we

push aside questions we are yet too boneheaded to answer, to attend to the ordinariness of bill paying and to what is normal come and go in our town of five thousand. For Xmas, I took an Electra out of my showroom and parked it in my driveway for Darlene to ooohhh over; on New Year's, at a party at Tommy Gaddy's ranch, I danced an ancient cha-cha-cha with Harriet Feltman and received for my efforts a knee sprain and two dozen hostile expressions from her husband Marv; in February I fired my disc-brakes expert for stealing tools and for using marijuana in the storeroom behind Parts. For three months, I say, I kept out of my mind any thoughts of Stacy and Buddy and the modern reflection they were of my long-gone Leonna and the distant me.

"You're a sick man," Fudge Walker told me more than once during this time. "What you need is a good drunk and five hours of golf."

When I was small and absorbed only with the idea of the rooting-tooting cowboy I wanted to be one day, my mother (this was much before my father shipped her up to Las Vegas to live with folks addicted to glue and pills and laundry pencils and vodka) used to insist that memory was a door—"a goddamn portal," her exact phrase was—to a room we entered like burglars or the otherwise naughty-minded. "You don't dare stay too long," she said. It is spookhouse, she said, and crypt and Oz and nailed-up closet—an idea she inherited, it is clear, from her lanky insurance-selling father and the oddball Louisiana-swampland Presbyterianism he practiced.

That's corny, I know—cheap as anything secondhand sold to us as new—but for me, as for all who accept cheapness as one fact of life, it works. The other day, for example, in my office, my shades drawn, my phone disconnected, what business I had (a new-car inventory, mostly) swept into a corner, I entered that memory room, through the "goddamn" it is, a zillion times. I

saw, and won again, my first serious fistfight (with the offensive
dufus Philip Trafton was). I saw the first car I drove, a Ford
Fairlane 500, and another I, drunk, spun off a highway overpass.
I saw a stubbly cotton field I lay in during a graduation party and
awakened again to the sight of my pal Les Fletcher hanging out
of the top of his convertible and steering with his bare feet. I
saw, and felt again, the important breasts of Mary Jo Griggs, and
watched her pat my hands as if to say I'd survive the need of her.
Most important, I stumbled again into that storehouse my
damaged mother grew moony over, and saw, shiny and real as
my own bald head, what is now a three-year-old image of
Leonna Allen, Texas registered nurse.

This was at the Pan American Center at New Mexico State
University, a good university whose not-good basketball team
was—on the night I peeked into again—taking on the drib-
blers and giants from the University of the Pacific. Buddy was
with me, partly overwhelmed by the ten thousand screamers
around us, and on the way back from the concession stand I
saw this Leonna I once upon a time loved, and was frozen by
the coincidence that fate is. "Lordy," I said. "Wait." This is
an old moment, like the noisy minutes in a bad movie or the
har-de-har-har of the community theater that Darlene regularly
drags me to. I want to say we made contact—through eyes and
beating hearts?—but we did not. I want to say a spotlight or
two shone on us, but they did not. Instead, I found my way
back to my seat, my feet like a puppet's, my head whipping left
and right trying to find her and not, at the same time, dump
my cherry Coke in the lap of a fanatic Aggie.

"What happened to you?" Buddy said when I sat down.

On the court, California's black men were clobbering ours.
In the stands, the fans were all worked up and angry, but higher
up and to the right, maybe where all crackpot visions are, was
flesh and hair and voice I once thought worth crying for.

"Leonna Allen," I said, pointing.

Buddy gave a look-see. He appeared serious. Then baffled. Then blank, like a fish. He'd heard the name before, but it was only a sound—like Zulu to an Eskimo—and not full of power and time and pain. So I told him.

Right there, amidst the riot defeat is and at a volume inconsistent with the privacy shame is, I gave him my history: the beginning and petered-out end it had, the songs I played for her (which were Lesley Gore and whiney as the pound-bred puppy Buddy currently has), the barbells I lifted to puff me up, the rented dinner jacket (with cummerbund) I wore to Cotillion. Because these events and feelings are as much features of my permanent record as the numbers America makes you live with and the names your parents have, I dumped the whole scribbled-on folder of me in front of him: the one sister-brother kiss we had in the marriage booth at the FFA fair, the shine her hair held, the singsong hello she had, what the bottom of me did when she made clear that Archie Freeman Mather was not at the center of the circle she was drawing. Then, winded by the effort, I asked, "You understand?"

He was bored. He was only book-smart. He was twelve. His old man was lunatic.

"Sure," he said. "Geez," he said. "Uh, thanks," he said.

And that would be all, I knew. Until his own life had been split, or burned up, or razed by the necessary catastrophe love is.

·   ·   ·

And so, after I came out of that unhappy funhouse of memory and before I discovered on I-25 what I was truly meant to know and to say about Buddy's first love and mine, I screwed up. I sought, at fitting times and not, to put my two cents in. At the dinner table, as the green beans went round and the conversation became the high-octane chitchat we enjoy, I'd hear a comment about women—or failure, or what an elected ding-dong in Santa Fe had said—and, given the two-plus-two-equals-five thinking I had, I'd see a way, wrong as cussing in church, of moving our talk to the subjects of youth and love.

I'd sputter, drop my fork with a bang, hum as the self-important do; and Darlene, former Zeta Tau pledge chairperson and Dona Ana County rodeo champion, would raise her tough eyes to mine and say, "Don't." In the TV room, hearing Hollywood's description of the battleground between boys and girls, I'd sit up like a judge, slam my mouth into gear; and my wife, with her master's degree in sociology and yellow belt in karate, would say, "Archie, don't." I heard that word, whispered and wailed, in the bathroom, in my smoky den, in the living room, on the patio. It reached me by phone, by note taped to the refrigerator, and once by Bucky Gridley (who approached me at the Fourth of July picnic to say, "Darlene says don't").

I even heard it one Saturday in August when Buddy and I were in the garage tending to the riding mower: I had stopped, a look to the eyes that is three-quarters schoolmarm; I had thought to say, once and for all, Whoa and Stop and Watch Out. Then Darlene hollered at me. "Don't you dare," she said. She was indoors, at the kitchen sink, her face half out the window, and my eyes went first to Buddy, who was greasy-fingered and sure enough happy, and then to the horizon, which was flat and empty and dark. "Archie Freeman Mather," she scolded. A dishcloth was waving. "Why don't you just leave him alone? He doesn't need to hear from you right now."

So I told other people, the near and not so near to me. I told Fudge Walker when we were at the Las Cruces Country

Club—specifically the nineteenth hole, which is golf for "booze and bullshit"—about how Buddy would have his heart ripped from him by Stacy Jeanne Toomer, first girlfriend. I told Fudge Walker, who was sloshed enough to listen and mumble affirmatively, about Buddy and the clumsy, inevitable two-step the end of his love would be. There would be phone calls and silences, eyeballs that flipped in and out of focus. In one week there would be giddiness, jokes whose humor rises from the belly of us; in the next, there would be that comic-book storm-cloud that forms over the head in ugly times. It was an old story, I said, the oooppps and aaarrgghhh of it, her lines and actions as familiar to me as his.

It was February, and I was talking to Harvey and Ella Sweem, who'd come in for a Skylark; then it was March, and I was telling Billie Jean Maxwell at the Farmers and Merchants Bank. "It's happening," I said, not at all pleased to be right. "You watch and see."

When it was time for woe, I say, woe came. As did—like the order A, B and C are—merriment and messiness and calamity. Buddy charged out and crept back, dragged out and hurtled back. In a manner that did not surprise, he was yappy and tight-lipped, generous as a poor man and stingy as a banker. It was, as my dead father liked to say, frick followed by frack. *If this*, I remembered from the philosophy I had dropped at SMU, *Then that.*

Then the end announced itself. This was a Wednesday, in the late evening. Darlene was in our bedroom, reviewing the work she does for our county welfare office, Craig John was asleep, and I was in my paper-strewn study, trying to see how much money I had. I heard the door and Buddy's footsteps and then my own voice say, "Well," which is one idiot word that occurs when knowledge comes our way.

Because, for all purposes practical in the melodrama this is,

I was my son himself—just removed from him by years and more brooding—I knew what was on his mind. As I had when Leonna Allen directed me to step over yonder, please, and never come back, Buddy had shut down. He was saying "God damn" to himself. And "Christ." And "Jesus H." He was outraged—he'd been bushwhacked, cheated and stomped. "Shit," he was saying. "Damn."

The kitchen door went crash, and I heaved up, told my legs to get moving. Halfway to the garage, where Buddy was heading, his Schwinn bicycle was flopped over, and I was going past a sweater I should have pulled on. My head was half here in time, half not. Part of me—the part that votes yellow-dog Democrat and tends to the buy-and-sell of living life—was watching another part, that which was itself once young and silly and in a hurry to grow up.

"Don't come in," Buddy said, when he heard my hand on the knob. "Just go away. You have nothing to say to me."

In there were tools it takes years to get the sense of, and trunks, and junk—bottles, rags, tin cans, stuff it takes four moves to accumulate. I knew he was still, studying himself, taking hold of the anger in him.

"I know what you're going to do," I said.

Between us was a standard hollow-core door, nothing at all to jam your fist through when everything has let you down.

"Yeah, you know everything," he said. "Just go away."

I'd done the same thing, I told him. Only it was my bedroom door, the very one *he* now slams when there is something personal to be tended to.

"So what?" he said. "Big deal."

Overhead was darkness, black upon black upon black, and way off a dog was howling to come in.

"You could bust a knuckle," I said, trying to be sensible. "Maybe your wrist."

A light had gone on inside, and the scrape of a boy's feet setting themselves.

"That means six weeks in a cast," I said. "No baseball."

"Who cares?" he snapped.

One of us had to do something, I told myself. A gesture had to be made, so I made it. I turned away, reminded myself where my wallet was, my car keys, how best to get to the hospital. I took one step, as if wobbling on a high wire, and another, all the while arranging what I'd say, in a minute or two, to Darlene about the connection between self-mangling and the excellent condition love is.

·　·　·　·

I like stories with morals: stories that say, "Here is the line and you may not cross it"; stories, written by anyone from the anywhere we live in, that make clear the hole the inner life pokes in the outer. Primitive attitude though it is, I like stories with folks you can root for (as you root for those in your own towns to be heroes and heroines). I like strength for the strong, ruin for the ruinous. Yet now—it is 11:37 P.M. (Mountain Standard Time), on a Thursday in the middle of December in the year of our Lord 1987—your storyteller can't say what it is he knew when these events were, well, fresh and not so picked over by memory. Time moves not forward, I think, but round and round and round until, when the heart is involved, there is no now or then; there is only turmoil with you in the center of it, like a stick.

I had my own end, in the assbackwards report this is, well before Buddy put his fist through my garage door. I had been in Albuquerque, at a convention, and was on my way home. Ours was the postcard spectacle of sunshine that New Mexico is the standard for, high heavens that discourage those words the "Range" song sings of. On my radio was the polite redneck music I go for, what can be yodeled through the nose about betrayal and getting caught. For a time, as I drove south, I had the feeling that those passing by me, high speed or not, were, whatever their station or point of view, my friends. I'd wave, or tip the Hibs and Hannon ten-gallon hat I wear out of town, and in answer would come a tractor-trailer's toot or what tourists from New Jersey think is a buckaroo's howdy.

As forward-feeling as are winning gamblers, I took note of my age, which is forty-three, and accepted the content I am. I thought of the fat I ought to lose, and the sweat involved in losing it. I thought of striped ties to look dandy in, and ostrich boots that take eight months to make, and how charitable the outlook of the homeward-bound is. And then, nodding over the notion of how much more than tissue and gore and skeleton we are, I thought of Buddy and what terrible event awaited him.

The floor fell out of me then, plank by plank by plank. Stunned—is there another word that says how dumb we wise guys can instantly become?—I took the one, two, three deep breaths my mother said were vital in crisis. "Geez," I said—the same expression my son used the night he heard my confession in Aggieland. "Well, I'll be damned," I said, and pinched myself wide awake to pull off the road like a responsible citizen. I switched the radio off, put my car in neutral, cranked down a window, and tried to light a cigarette. Left and right and front and back of me stretched the desert I like so much, a wrinkled, scrub-dotted outland not so inhospitable as many imagine. Ahead, down a dip or two, lay the towns of Lemitar, and Socorro, and Truth or Consequences, and way, way off— where it was already less light—was my home in Hatch. I was thinking of Buddy, how skinny he is and the too-tight jeans he wears. He was in love now, I was thinking, and would be one day not. He was happy now, and would be one day not.

"Lordy," I said. It was a word that had no meaning, just a sound to be made in a big, empty place. I had a thought about love, which made no sense, and another, about the pieces to be picked up afterward. "Okay," I told myself. "Five minutes," I said. I had a cigarette to smoke and one or two more facts to know, then I'd stop thinking, put my car in gear, and go home.

The other victim the summer my wife left me was my dreamlife, which, like a mirage, dried up completely the closer we came to the absolute end of us. In the fourteen years we were married, I had been a ferocious dreamer, drawing all I knew or feared or loved about the waking world into my sleeplife. If I had seen a neighbor's animal—Les Fletcher's horse, say, or Newt Grider's collie dog—in my dreams that night I would see dozens of them, beasts whose language I understood and respected, animals whose own stories I heard and weeped over just as one day I would weep over my private misfortune.

One night—actually the early-morning hours after our first son was born—I watched a flock of pigeons from my wife's hospital room. There were hundreds, mindless as those swivel-eyed birds can be, flapping and swirling in a hurly-burly over the massive air conditioners, their bird-chatter an unhappy, loud whirring, constant as party talk. It was a noise I heard

distinctly hours later when I fell asleep at home. They were
yammering, those dreambirds; and what they said to each
other, and would say to others yet to arrive, seemed so sensible
to me in my sleep that I awoke smiling, as if I had heard secrets
vital enough to live by. I had been where they had been—north
and south, in good weather and bad—all the places they visit,
into trees and onto ledges, on rooftops and in parks. I was, in
the few hours I dozed, a pigeon.

Another time, on a vacation to Disneyland, I became the
folks we met on the road—those who pumped our gas, or
cooked burgers for us, or stood behind the desks at the Holiday
Inns we stayed in. I was the boy who bussed our table in
Phoenix, the blonde woman outside the entrance of the San
Diego Zoo whose own child was colicky or too well-fed; I was
the motorists we passed by at sixty miles an hour, and I was
those citizens whose communities we circled on the atlas:
Santa Barbara, Laguna Beach, San Mateo. I paid their utility
bills (PG&E, water and garbage), shopped and ate and hollered
for them. At the end of our four weeks, as we drove south from
San Francisco to our home in Las Cruces, I was even the pilots
overhead, whose lingo was as remarkable and private as that,
yes, spoken by birds.

But when Karen left, my dreams stopped—not abruptly, as
if the tape that was my inner life had finally ended, but gradu-
ally, as if the world inside were subject to erosion by the
common elements of wind and water, and by the uncommon
elements of lovelessness and despair. My first night alone, I was
a general—a George Armstrong Custer. I had blond heroic
hair, plus heavy gold braid on a tight broadcloth tunic that
flattened the lazy-man's belly I have. My dream voice was
stern, gifted as what stage actors aim for, and for that voice I
used a vocabulary as fancy and important as one in any school-
book. In that dream, I issued orders which were ungrudgingly

obeyed and had my name called so often that, when my alarm
clanged, I woke saying, "Yes, how may I help?" I remember
standing—at attention, I suppose—at my bedside, alert as a
sentinel, listening for what was needed of me, what emergency
had fetched me into daylight again. "Karen?" I said. "What
is it?" I was awake, but part of me—that part, clearly, that
Karen had left when she went to her sister's in El Paso—part
of me believed that she was still here, if not in the bathroom
next door then in the kitchen.

Searching for her, I opened Danny's door, and then that of
Mark, his younger brother. Their bedrooms seemed empty, not
abandoned. Beds were made, closets organized, their toys put
away. Still, hearing her name over and over in my memory, I
looked for her. Her plants were here—the Boston fern, the
overwatered rhododendron—as were her books and most of her
clothes, but she was not; and it was only when I opened the
patio door and stood in the backyard, studying the rank of rose
bushes she'd planted the year before, that I snapped to. I had
been slugged, I felt. I was actually staggered, thrown backward
by a force like horror. "Karen?" I said again, but by then I did
not mean it. Her name was only a word given to an object that
wasn't here anymore. It was a word that stood for an absence,
like darkness itself, that had made way for the waking life.

In the weeks that followed, my dreams came quickly, but
with parts missing or poorly joined. They had no beginnings
and their endings seemed less like conclusions than, well, inter-
ruptions. Not nightmares exactly, they were like slide exhibits,
flashing picture shows thrown together by the weary, unthink-
ing heart of me. The family came and went: my boys were
born, grew, and went into adulthood in minutes. My father,
dead many years, appeared dressed for golf, in the too-colorful
plus fours he favored, and in his happy Panama hat. He did not
speak, nor did I see him, as I often had, in front of the TV,

his expression fixed and baleful. Instead, he was swinging his Walter Hagen driver, in slide after slide, his stroke an enviable display of coordination and strength. I saw my mother too. In every frame that rose out of the night, she sat at the the shallow end of the country club pool, her bathing suit an unflattering one-piece affair whose wide shoulder straps hung down her arms and whose skirt seemed more appropriate to a child. She was fluttering her feet in the water, again and again and again, and pointing, in obvious joy, to a soaked figure in the baby pool—me, I think—a skinny, clumsily diapered toddler. One night I saw the few friends I had as a youngster—Mark Runyan, John Risner, Jay Bullard—and I saw the first house we lived in, 111 West Gallagher, behind which was a cotton field where we raced our Schwinn bicycles and, later, a rusted two-door Ford we bought. I saw the girl I loved first, a high school sophomore named Michelle Parker, and I saw the way she was now, which was sad and too perplexing to sleep through. I saw the Texas college I could not graduate from, the cramped dorm room I lived in, and the Lake Dallas oil man's house I was violently drunk in once. And often, too often to be unimportant, I saw faces and events placed side by side, as if between them I were to make comparisons; as if between, on the left, my wife at home in her nightwear, and on the right, me in the caddy room at the country club, I were to see a connection.

I saw nothing. No meaning, no significance. I was uninvolved, as distant from what was being shown to me in sleep as from what I had once seen in time. In these days, I climbed into bed after the ten-o'clock news, and before setting the alarm and switching off the bedstand light, I asked myself what silliness, what oddball's concoction of delight and misery, I would dream. Nothing of my job as a ninth-grade math teacher came to me, nor did I recognize anyone from the present—not Herb Swetman, my principal and best pal; not Emily Probert,

his secretary; not any of the youngsters I coach on the fresh-
man soccer team. Puzzled and partly stunned, I conceived of
my unconscious, the thing we are told our dreams spill from,
as a fishing net whose weave was too wide for the current world.

By September, my dreams involved me in tasks. Night after
night, I picked up leaves from trees I don't have, one by one,
and stacked them in piles as high as my ears. I wrote my name,
with one hand then the other, in ink and in pencil, on ruled
and on unlined paper. One time, after a phone call from Karen
(a conversation whose last lines were so impersonal they could
have been uttered by Martians), I sleepwalked. My dream
concerned thirst, and when the alarm went off, on my night-
stand I found not one but five glasses of water; and I report to
you now that I drank each of them, slowly and seriously, as if
I dared not, as if the penalty for neglecting what our dreams
bid us do is not less than death itself. Yes, I drank them; and
after each, in the silent moment between the putting down of
one and the taking up of another, I had a vision of myself as
I was when Karen and I married—an eager beaver ignorant of
what time can do to love.

The last of these dreams—when they ran out and never
came back—was almost a year later, after our divorce was final
and I knew I ought to go forward again. This was several years
ago, when I regularly played stud poker in the men's locker at
the country club. There were five of us, all married but me, and
the most you could lose in our quarter-limit game was twenty
dollars; we would drink and order roast beef sandwiches from
the second-floor snack bar and, if we planned to be late, we
could shower or, as we once did, we could dive into the pool
or go out to the driving range to be crazy. On the night of this
dream, I was the last to leave. I'd won, but the sight of my
winnings, folding money and change, didn't impress me. There
was no place to go. Ed had driven home to Bonnie, Max to

Jean, the rest to their wives, and I was there, in a chair, a drink at my elbow, listening to the showers drip and the satisfying musical whoosh-whoosh the outdoor sprinklers made.

Almost directly, I went to the pool and tumbled in, clothes and lace-up shoes and all, and as I had as a kid, I pulled straight for the deep end, down fifteen feet to the drain where, for the child I recalled, the pressure and heavy silence of the water overhead seemed as reassuring as gravity. Several times I plunged down, suspending myself as long as I could before crawling up for air. I felt good, I say. I had a wife who lived elsewhere, sons who would not be too much damaged by what had happened, and a job I was fine enough at; more important, I had this night to myself—a spread of stars whole nations could wish upon, and clouds that say rain is on the way, and breezes that bring with them the smells of what we plant hereabouts in the Mesilla Valley. I think I sang; or I wish I had sung, and now—in the wistful half of me that's putting this on paper—I hear that singing again, as if I were out on the course at night, and say to myself, as a stranger, that there is a man singing over yonder, in a scratchy voice that certainly has some liquor and cigarettes in it, and that man is happy.

I folded my soggy clothes over the chain-link fence and, alone like one of the first smart creatures on our planet, I considered this place. I studied the buildings—the pro shop, the ballroom, the women's locker a floor above our own—and beyond them, the third of my town that wasn't asleep or had no work to do. I could see Hiebert's Drive-In, the Rocket Theater, and the curve of North Main Street that swept by the Loretto Shopping Center. I could hear cars, faint and steady, and I wondered who was out there. I imagined moving the one hill in front of me and being able to point out the house I owned as well as those I pass every day on my way to Alameda Junior High School. I was putting together my world as my dreams had once put me together, and everywhere I looked I spotted something—a willow tree, someone's Lincoln Continental, a garage—that might look better over there. Or there. Or there. Naked, common sense stripped away by the Jack Daniel's booze I like, I saw the world I could construct for the sixty thousand souls I share it with. A house became a castle; a streetlight, a tower. I put X with Y, A with B, and by the time, an hour later, I sat down in a ratty chaise by the pool, this largest town in Dona Ana County had become as quaint and patchwork as those we yearn for from olden times that never were. Joy—and mirth and bliss and virtue—had many faces that night, I say; for I put in pockets or hearts or minds whatever over time had been stolen or broken or made sad.

And then I dreamed.

. . .

We are told, I believe, too many truisms about our inner lives. In books, magazines and on TV, in all the yakety-yak that comes our way, we hear too much about the selves we are. We are good, we hear, or we are bad; like dogs, or not; like angels, or not; flawed, or perfected. Our swamis tell us—preachers and teachers, politicians and doctors, all the tattling experts loose among us. But it is in dreams—of pigeons, of the past, of people long gone—that we attend to the inner life itself, hear it in its own words, at its own pitch.

My last dream featured the desert we have, the thousands of square miles of sand and rock and scrawny brush that doomsayers tell us will one day be your home too. It was a flat world, infertile as a skillet, with lightning flashing at the horizon. It was a world of red and yellow and green skies, all the colors poets love, a place whose light was liquid and melting all around. I was in it, I dreamed, at an unmarked crossroads, the age I am now, thirty-nine, and in good health. I could go left, or right, or straight, but to the man I was then, the choice made no real difference. I was to see something, I knew, and soon enough it appeared in the shimmering, indistinct distance. I was seeing myself out there, black against white, too tall in an otherwise diminished land. "All right," I said. "All right." And I waited—waited on me. My inner life, the world constructed from what I'd been or done, was speaking to me, patiently and calmly. I would hear what it had to say, and I would under-stand. And so I came to myself—observed the man I am now walk forward to the man I was then and take him, as you take your children, into his arms. The one held the other—the future cradling the present—and the one who had been left, the one whose interior hooks and hasps and snaps had come undone, gave himself up utterly. They were both there, in dreamland, under heaven and over hell, two versions of the same man, clasped in an embrace that would end when the world came up again.

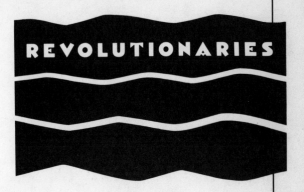

REVOLUTIONARIES

Long before he turned radical and disappeared into that "underground" we once upon a time used to hear so much about—and much before he showed up in my life again—Jimmy Spalding and I were best friends.

As kids we swam the flumes, the irrigation canal that passes over a railroad trestle where my father's farm—now my own—backs up to the levee for the Rio Grande River north of Las Cruces. At Alameda Junior High, the only middle school in what was then a town of ten thousand, we co-captained our bowling team, The Flying Aces, one of whose trophies I still have in a closet somewhere. In the ninth grade, we climbed C Mountain, dragging my mutt, Raleigh, along, and from a cliff thousands of feet higher than any bush in our desert, we turned our backs on what we knew was Hicksville to watch clouds churn our way from the Wonderland we'd heard California was.

"Going out there," Jimmy said. "Soon as I get my driver's license. You and me, pal. Do the whole scene, the beach trip."

In those days we aimed to be surfers. Or astronauts. Or truckers. We had the healthy fantasy life of all teenagers—a dreamlife composed of open space and money and women from the pages of *Nugget* and *Gent* magazines. We smoked cigarettes and talked tough and brought other guys—Jay Bullard and Mark Runyan—into a club that became part Three Musketeers, part Three Stooges. We'd watch the Bowery Boys at Jimmy's house, in the rec room his father had built after they bought the American Linen Supply firm. We joined the wrestling team, me at 136, Jimmy at 144. One month we read everything by Leon Uris—especially *Battle Cry,* which, when I've looked at it since, seems nothing like the WW II Sherwood Forest that I remember. We saw *Psycho* at the State Theater and a week later read *Last Exit to Brooklyn,* which Jimmy declared was art with all the gland left in.

"I'm meant to do something," Jimmy would say. "I got a real relationship with destiny."

Then, the summer after we graduated, in '66, as if one of us had died, we stopped being friends. I went for a National Thespian conference at the University of Indiana, stayed on for a course in the drama I still enjoy, and did not hear from him for two months.

"How come you didn't answer my letters?" I said in August. "I called three or four times, too. Your dad said he didn't know where you were."

"Been on the move, man." He shrugged. "San Francisco, Telegraph Hill, the VDC—the whole works."

He was standing inside his door, more in shadow than out.

"It's all coming together," he was saying. "Rock 'n' roll, the race thing, Vietnam. It's a process, Buddy. Medgar Evers, Reverend King, Bob Dylan."

I had planned to tell him about the kid I'd met at IU,
Morgan Maxwell, whose father was a VP with Kemper insurance. Morg had said that maybe the company plane would take
us all—Jimmy too, I'd insisted—to the Rose Bowl that winter.

"No can do," Jimmy said. "I got priorities now."

Sunlight was flying off a thousand surfaces, dizzying and
sharp.

"I'll come back tomorrow," I told him. "We'll see a movie,
go up to the club."

"Better not," he said. "I'm real busy. Got many things to
do."

"After school starts, then?"

We were going to the local college, New Mexico State
University, a deal we'd agreed to the September before.

"Yeah," he said. "That could be a real possibility."

I was trying to keep my mouth shut and back up at the same
time. This wasn't Jimmy, I was thinking. This wasn't anybody
I knew at all.

"Listen, man," he said, "I'll call you, okay? I got to
straighten some things out first, serious head stuff."

So that fall we left for what I know now are two different
worlds: me to that future opened up by Econ 102, Range
Management, and the *Principles of Organic Chemistry* by
Petry and Wallace; Jimmy to the fractured present revealed to
him by the *Evergreen Review,* Alan Watts, Jim Morrison and
the Doors. I'd spot him every now and then, a figure moving
alone and always upstream against the seven thousand shitkickers and jocks and sorority girls we undergraduates were. In
front of Corbett Center one time I saw him handing out
leaflets—a broadside from Senator George McGovern of
South Dakota: "Who really appointed us God for people elsewhere around the world?"

"Long time," I told him. "How's it going?"

"Great," he said. "Got work to do, my man. Minds to change, hearts to heal."

He had a pile of dead-baby pictures—napalmed, he said—and a smile that had little to do with making Bs in Intro to Sociology.

"You really believe this stuff, don't you?"

"Abso-goddamn-lutely," he said. "You ought to join us, Buddy. We have no rules and everybody sleeps late."

Walking around us as if we both had the plague were kids who wanted to be doctors or mechanical engineers or state lawmakers or teachers—plain college kids who, I hoped, would one day be my friends and neighbors.

"Sorry," I told him. "If I knew what to do, I'd do it, honest."

"Man," Jimmy was saying, "you're young, you can be like me. I got it knocked, Buddy. I say what I want, smoke a little dope, it's paradise."

That October I heard that Jimmy intended to march on the Pentagon with Joan Baez. I learned, too, that he'd burned his draft card to send the ashes to General Hershey. In April of '68, before Johnson ended the bombing in North Vietnam, I found an essay, "Liberation from the Affluent Society," clipped under the windshield wiper of my truck.

"Read this shit, man," an attached note said. "Essential knowledge herein. Dig the part on mechanisms of manipulation and repression." He'd signed his initials inside a peace symbol. "It's like the man said," Jimmy had scrawled, " 'Rise up and abandon the creeping meatball.' "

That summer I worked for my father—chopping cotton, running the cultivator, odd jobs—and spent my free time at the country club. I didn't see Jimmy until I ran into him outside Young Hall, the English building, the next semester.

"What're you taking?" he wondered.

"Lit survey," I said. "Keats, Byron, those guys."

"I approve," he said. "The revolutionaries, first-rate. Broaden the mind, let the light shine in."

His hair hung long now, braided in the back, and watching his face was very hard work. He was pale too, as if he'd spent three months in a closed room.

"I talked to your dad a couple times," I said. "He said you'd disappeared."

"Big rally next month," he said. "You ought to show up. "We'll get stoned, do miracles outrageous. It'll be highly provocative."

I thought about my own father, particularly the happy noises he made about Nixon, and what Mr. Agnew was calling an "effete corps of impudent snobs." Plus I had a girlfriend, Mary Jane Byrd, a Chi Omega who would one day be my wife for several years and part of the reason I'm telling this.

"I got classes," I said. "Maybe I'll watch."

He nodded, and I felt old—less his pal than his enemy.

"I like the hat," he said. "You're gonna make one hell of a cowboy, Buddy."

For three straight weeks his name was in the *Round-Up*, the student newspaper. He even made the *Sun News*, the local daily. He was quoted often and with what seemed like considerable care. He called for upheaval and anarchy, a repudiation of mindless affluence. He mentioned H. Rap Brown and the SDS, as well as what Fidel Castro was said to have accomplished.

"You know this guy, don't you?" Mary Jane said to me once.

She'd worked a year in Up With People and had a cheerful disposition I couldn't get enough of. What's more, she planned to be a TV newscaster and I wanted to be around when the world saw how beautiful she was.

"Well," she said, "I think he's an idiot."

I was there that Friday, part of the curious who watched nearly two dozen students and faculty and lonely townsfolk

march across the steps of the administration building. They
were what motley is: waving signs, they shouted, "Hell, no, we
won't go!" and Jimmy led them in a speech that used language
like "oppression" and "imperialism" and "colonialism"—all
the words and habits of mind, he has since told me, we have
to learn anew every time there is murder and public suffering
in an acre of the world we own.

"We want ROTC off campus," he hollered once. "We want
Bob Hope off TV and Frank Sinatra out of the movies." He
waved his hands. "We want classes in nudity."

Toward the end—before the campus cops and four state
policemen broke it up by dragging Jimmy off—he delivered a
rambling, singsongy declaration that mentioned Abe Maslow,
Aldous Huxley, Carl Rogers, D. T. Suzuki—names that passed
over me like clouds. They were the dead or the living, or the
never-were. I wanted him to talk—if that's all this was—about
being afraid, about what dead William Wordsworth's verse
skills had to do with anything, and about what I was supposed
to be doing in five or ten years. But he went on—"We're
discussing human worth here!"—his hair flyaway, his T-shirt
too small and covered with buttons, his cheeks painted like an
Apache's, ignoring the hecklers who said he was queer, or
chickenshit, or a commie.

"And now," he announced, "in keeping with the theatrical
theme of today's lesson, I will piss on this wall."

Instantly, a state policeman, a sergeant named Krebs who is
now an official of our Dona Ana County, burst out of the door
behind Jimmy, and the scene was like two minutes of Walter
Cronkite's evening news: words were exchanged, an official
arm snatched my friend by the neck, and I woke up to see him
spread-eagled on the pavement, facedown, blood oozing from
one ear.

"We'll surround this place," Jimmy was shouting. "We'll be

holy men, chanting and beating drums, and this place will rise
into the air. At three hundred feet all the evil spirits will fall
out!"

Every time I play this moment in my memory, I see myself
interfering—honorably and fearlessly; I am strong, in this
dream world I construct, and I am angry. I act righteously, like
Superman or one loudmouth world-beater Jimmy believed in.
I do not stand, as I did, beside my girlfriend, Mary Jane Byrd
and shake, breathing hard. I do not watch my friend yanked
away, one arm twisted behind his back.

"I hate this sort of thing," Mary Jane Byrd said. "Whenever
I hear about it, I just close my eyes and pretend."

A couple of hours later, I visited him in a private room on
the second floor of Memorial General Hospital.

"Your dad told me where to find you," I said.

He was sitting up in bed, wearing a hospital nightgown, a
knot of gauze around his head, one eye swollen shut in a pulp
of blue and yellow flesh. The room had eight shades of white
and the half-dozen hairs on his chin made him look feeble,
stupid.

"Big man, my father," Jimmy was saying. "Pulled some
strings, I gather. Asked me if I was concerned about my reputa-
tion, about a job. Man, I don't want a job."

In a chair beneath the wall-mounted TV sat a girl I'd never
seen before. She was dark as an Indian, plus fleshy in a way that
made you think about sex first.

"That's Carla," Jimmy said. "We're sort of going together.
It's antirevolutionary, I guess, very retrograde. I see us having
lots of babies."

She made a point of ignoring the hello I offered.

"Gonna run some errands," Carla said, getting up. "I'll
catch you later."

"Classic bohemian," Jimmy said after she left. "She's from

Parsipanny, New Jersey. Came down here to molest ag students and be an agitator. We have a real spiritual thing."

Out the window I could see traffic on Water Street. Directly across stood the Papen Building, an improbable ten-story bank and office tower whose basement Jimmy and I had explored when it was going up years before. We'd been in its vault, all its secret rooms.

"Some scene, huh?" Jimmy said. "Man, what a rush the violence is. They wanted to rip my face off, 3-D Apocalypse. I was quoting Che Guevara in the cop car."

We were going to break, I was thinking. There was nothing between us anymore—not music we liked, not stories, not anything to think about.

"You lost a tooth," I told him.

He smiled. "I like the hole. Has symbolic value."

We used to fish for carp in the tide pools of the Rio Grande. Carrying pointed bamboo or cottonwood branches, we'd sprint up and down, slapping the water and howling. I was thinking of that and where we used to hide the Pall Mall cigarettes we'd swiped from my father.

"You ever try LSD?" Jimmy asked.

In my mind, I was already out the door, putting between us then all the time and distance I feel now about these events.

"I'm really disappointed in you," he said. "You'd be so much more interesting as a leftist."

                          .   .   .

For James Edward Spalding, I now understand, violence as a way of life started the day the citizens of Rush Springs, Oklahoma, voted to outlaw public dancing. "That was the last damn straw," he'd said. "After I heard that, I knew I wasn't dealing with the rational. I was into Oz." While I was being graduated and married (plus joining Kiwanis and our country club), and managing the farm and doing musicals like *Guys and Dolls* and *The Music Man* at our community theater in La Mesilla, Jimmy was drifting outward and sinking, moving— so he admitted three days ago—underground, marching and protesting, going to jail, learning about machine pistols and pipe bombs that can be concocted from kerosene and guano. In fifteen years, while I was buying this and that, and planting onions and then lettuce and then chilies, and watching the world zoom by in a haze, Jimmy was going deeper and further and quieter. In the fifteen years between that day in the hospital and the night he appeared in my kitchen, while he was building a foot-thick file in the National Security Agency and whirling unpredictably under America, I was losing my dad to pancreatic cancer and my mom to the drink, and divorcing and waking up every month, or year, to drink Old Grand-Dad and marvel at the quiet loneliness I was living in.

"There's no movement anymore," he confessed that night. "Just free-lancers. We wander, my friend. That's what I do: I drift and live off my anger."

I'd been at the men's locker room at the country club, playing stud poker, and when I got home, something in the air—"the big mystery that is the twentieth century," Jimmy would say—told me I was not alone. My hair stood up on the back of my neck, I prepared myself to beat the holy Jesus out of the dipstick who was trying to rob me, and then I saw him drinking coffee at my breakfast table, and right away, in all the beating organs I have, I was pleased he was here.

"Hope you don't mind," he said. "I made myself at home. We old-time hippies consume a lot of caffeine. Keeps the edges sharp. Gotta stay one jump ahead of the bad guys."

"How'd you get in?"

His was Br'er Rabbit's goofy grin. "Magic. Hocus-pocus

from the criminal elements, plus an American Express credit card."

He looked like a banker at a bowling alley: a good taxpayer's haircut and black horn-rimmed glasses that gave me the impression he had something to lose. He was gray at the temples and too tan for the March we'd had.

"Who mashed your nose?"

It was bent like those we've seen in the *Godfather* movies.

"Plastic surgery," he said. "Had a mole removed, too. Very hush-hush."

He'd been gone and now he was back and for an hour he explained how he'd come here. Until the surgery he'd used a wig he'd bought at the Max Factor School for Makeup in Hollywood. He'd taken classes at Kansas State University. He'd been a pen pal with the IRA's James McCann. He'd met Kunstler, written for *Overthrow* magazine, one time walked into the Rahway penitentiary in New Jersey, been hooked up with the Peace and Freedom Party. The names came and went: Las Vegas, Habana, Chicago, Sulphur Springs, Florida. He'd even bunked at an SLA house owned by Donald DeFreeze.

"That man did a thousand push-ups a day," Jimmy said. "He was once cornered by a cop with a police dog. Field Marshal Cinque was real pleasant until he snapped that dog's neck."

I asked a farm boy's question about Patty Hearst. Something was up. As in the old days, we'd get to it in a minute, or an hour.

"Nice lady," he said. "Not the sort to get nervous in a crowd."

He'd spent one summer in St. Thomas, learned to scuba dive, and he entertained the idea of becoming a deep-water laborer for Shell Oil in the North Sea. He'd attended a rock festival in Puerto Rico. "Saw Black Sabbath on Easter Sunday," he said. "A bad scene—knife fights, too hot, rapes, no medics. That's when I knew it had turned serious."

I was thinking of my own life—bacon and eggs, the price of dry fertilizer, the Agriculture Department Block runs, where my mind went when the sun went down. Jimmy was right: life was serious, and I had the two slipped discs and one tiny ulcer to prove it.

"Met Dr. Spock once," Jimmy was saying. "He did a physical for my daughter, Ruthie. That man makes a mean banana daiquiri."

"You're married."

"Exactly," he said. "This is a very straight, nearly Republican child I have. She's a champ, not like us at all."

A name came to me from the long-ago days: "Carla."

He nodded and I had time enough to study this man who, I would learn, remains of real interest to the FBI for such activities as bank robbery, interstate flight to avoid prosecution, possession of explosives, assault, resisting arrest—a thousand antisocial incidents that make fascinating reading in the Water Street Post Office. A kid, I said to myself. A wife.

"What're you doing here, Jimmy?"

The silence went on enough to be important.

"Actually, I'm not going to be here long—you don't need to know where I'm going—but I need a favor."

I was concentrating on my coffee cup—how hot it was, how old. It had elephants in different positions that looked like sex, a gift from Mary Jane Byrd, and was meant to be the first funny thing we'd see in the morning.

"I'm meeting Carla," he said. "She and Ruth are driving over here from Tucson."

"That's where they live?"

"It doesn't matter where they live, Buddy. We do this reunion bit pretty frequently, a sentiment thing. I thought you wouldn't mind."

I took note of what is heard hereabouts at two in the morning: the wind, a wall clock, my mostly paid-for house taking its own pulse, the Fletchers' three-legged shepherd in their onion field.

"There's something else, isn't there?"

"We'll be out by daybreak," he said. "Maybe a little later."

Eight at the latest, I told him. My loan officer, Victor Fears, from the Citizen's Bank was coming out at nine. I had a pile of debt and, at the moment, only a half-dozen payment books to show for it.

"Right on, Buddy," Jimmy said. "I knew I could count on you."

"I'm doing a lot of dumb stuff lately."

He stood at the stove now, and it was nothing to see him as he was at fifteen—too skinny through the chest, full of jokes about what a smooth operator he was.

"You're like me, man," he was saying. "I stole all my ideas from the Lone Ranger—goodness against evil and injustice. And never shoot to kill."

.   .   .

An hour later we sat in my Buick station wagon outside his old house on Amador Street so he could teach me about the property fetish that underlies genocidal war. His old house stood dark (his dad had died two years earlier), almost concealed by new landscaping, and Jimmy was telling me that it—the olden times, the hard rain, the winds Bob Dylan sang about—was coming back.

"Nicaragua," he said. "Salvador, people in the streets."

I had mentioned what Mary Jane Byrd said men were—

which had to do with not looking around yourself carefully and being pig-headed in matters of the heart.

"What's it feel like?" I asked.

He was looking at his hands as if they held a surprise for him. "The violence," I said. "What's it like?"

"You get used to it," he said. "You abstract, invent stories."

In Jimmy's old house lived the Whittiers, a family I'd met twice and now seemed connected to by something deeper than happenstance or the running forward of our lives.

"First time," he said, "I wet my pants. The rush was incredible, just movement and light and voices. Then everybody— the citizens, Ma and Pa Kettle—everybody does what you say. It's hard to understate a feeling like that."

His words were piling up like stones.

"It used to be fun, a party."

"And now?"

He shrugged.

"Now it's work, a job." He had a cigarette going. "Sometimes I have to remind myself what it's for, who the enemy is."

The silence had shape and substance. Between us was not space but time, what the years had made. We had been brought together again—yes, like magic—but between us, as between planets, was only space we might holler across.

"I get tired," he was saying. "Sometimes I don't know who I am."

I knew that feeling, I thought.

"A fugitive's brain is filled with data," he was saying. "A hundred names, numbers, lots of ID. Revolution requires a first-class memory."

He told me he'd been L. Manning Vines, from Sioux City, Iowa; blood type O; born August 13, 1948. And Archie Felts from Atlanta, whose father was Ira, whose mother was Velma, who had brothers named Bert and Maxwell. The invented past

piled up: a hundred jobs, a deck of Social Security cards, made-
up work records, biographies borrowed from *Seize the Day* and
The Old Curiosity Shop, surnames from the *Guinness Book of
World Records.* Everything was faked: whole families imagined, breathed into life for an interview, a license check. "I got
a whole population in my head," he said. Family trees that
stretched back to England and France and goddamn Holland,
a story that put him in one place and not another, mirages he
inhabited for an hour, a month, a bus ride. Part of him belonged to an Elks club in Missouri, another to a YMCA Big
Brothers program in Columbus, Ohio. He was a fifth-grade
teacher, a bricklayer in Union City. A part of him—a part as
impossible as men on Mars—owed money; a part had stock in
BioGen.

"I've even been you," he said. "For two days a long time ago,
I was Joe Benson Neville, Jr. You were a mean son of a bitch
then, Buddy, but you were exceedingly happy."

I understood then, why he was really here: as if it had already
happened, as if I'd already read the newspapers or watched the
six-o'clock broadcast from KTSM in El Paso, I could see the
smoke, the confusion, a person like me going whichaway in a
daze.

"Where?" I said.

"Close," he said. "Very close."

I took a second, attended to the thud my heart made and
how my breathing worked.

"Nobody'll get hurt, right?" I asked. "This is important to
me."

A car drove by and his face filled up with light—a new nose,
shapes from a geometer's mind, what emotion is.

"A few hours from now," he began, "an invented PFC
creature named Blocker from Peoria, Illinois, will strike a blow
for the Great Blah-Blah-Blah. It will be dramatic, telegenic,

but very modest in terms of property loss. It's the eighties, man, blood isn't the issue anymore."

I had the car started. We could go now, I thought. Or we could still be here when the sun came up. I had the sensation that I was outside, perhaps in the room of Jimmy's old house, where the Whittiers now slept, watching. My ex-wife came to mind, Mary Jane Byrd, and the long-limbed Chevrolet dealer she'd taken up with. I felt fifteen years roll up and unfurl, leading me back in a rush.

"Let's go home," I said.

. . .

Near four A.M. a car came up my dirt road from Highway 85, a four-door Ford so plain I thought I'd seen it everywhere. "Carla," Jimmy said. He'd been pacing for the last hour, quiet and deliberate, field-stripping his smokes. I'd asked him once about the ditty bag he'd dropped beside me on the steps. It was GI stuff, olive drab, official. "Tools of the trade," he'd said. "I'm a True Believer, sad to say." Now he walked over, his face blank, a sober man with earnest mission, and picked up the bag.

"We'll be back in two hours," he said. "Three at the outside. Ruthie'll stay here."

Behind the wheel sat Carla, my garage light too bright in her eyes. I was thinking about my dog, Raleigh, which had been run over, and what she might say about that. Behind her, another. Ruthie. The passenger door opened. All right, I was thinking. Okay. And then Jimmy was inside, his Everyman's Ford accelerating quietly toward the highway.

"You must be Mr. X," the girl said. "Daddy's real secretive about these things, so don't tell me your name, okay?"

I felt something dry and small, possibly bonelike, break free inside.

"I'm Ruth," she said, extending her hand. "I had a name from the revolution, Little Star, but Carla says public schools aren't ready for a whole lot of poetry yet."

She was fourteen or so, and too much like a nighttime-TV teenager to be looked at straight on—the windblown hair that is said to be popular nowadays and eye makeup that maybe covers up the inner life.

"I take it you know what they're up to," I said.

"I'm in the ninth grade," she said, "I stay in my room, or hang out with kids I know. I don't know anything."

We watched their taillights go south on the highway until a semi with its brights on passed us too fast going the other way.

"So what's on our agenda?" she wondered.

In an hour—after a breakfast I made and the dishes she washed—we sang "Pink Shoe Laces" by Dody Stevens, "Great Balls of Fire" by Jerry Lee Lewis, "If I Didn't Care" by Connie Francis, "Good Golly, Miss Molly" and "No Other Arms, No Other Lips"—songs I had been collecting ever since my father died and the house became mine. I don't know how we got from A to Z—from knowing about terror to knowing what old-time music says about love—but in one hour the big world vanished and we took up residence in the smaller world of broken hearts and expensive 45s. Once she learned the lyrics, Ruthie was terrific, unafraid to throw open the mouth and just yowl when the feeling hit. She even insisted I play the bongos Mary Jane Byrd had bought years ago; and I, exhilarated and cut free for a time, banged away like a dervish, until Ruthie said, between records falling on my turntable, that she couldn't wait to get out, go away.

"I have it all planned," she said. "After I graduate, I'm going to Iowa maybe—a real small college."

On the record player, the King, Elvis Presley, was telling us about his blue suede shoes.

"They don't know, do they?"

She shook her head. "I get these quizzes at home. They make me read *The Nation* and *Commonweal* and *Mother Jones*. I'm supposed to save the world, they say. Go to Berkeley. Be there when the shitstorm comes again. They started taking me on these trips last year."

She was going to cry.

"You want me to turn them in, don't you?"

"Daddy said you wouldn't. Said you were a cool guy."

I took in the character of my living room: the La-Z-Boy I sleep in, the Motorola TV I watch too much of, the Woolworth's guitar I sometimes play when I need Merle Haggard's view of things.

"What'd Carla say?"

"She said you were retrograde, completely coopted. That's the way she talks. Said you were bourgeoisie, no balls."

My heart did a strange turn, a twist on its thick root.

"Maybe she's right," I said.

So we waited. We sat on the steps where her father and I had waited, and watched the new day come up—a day that would be hot and clear all the way to heaven. I had my eyes on the Organ Mountains to the east—the San Augustin Pass, near where they'd tested the Apollo rockets—jagged purple spears of bare rock behind which, if my guess was correct, Jimmy and Carla would now being doing their business at the MAR site in the desert missile range. I'd driven past it many times—on my way to ski in Cloudcroft, or to picnic at the national monument at White Sands—a bubble of glass a thousand yards north of the two-lane highway, miles and miles of unguarded flatland around it; inside, from what I'd heard, was

a radar arrangement that offered a view of the skies from
California to Alabama. It was an eye that missed nothing from
above, and I wondered who had built such a thing and who
would care if a bomb went off near it.

"I'm not going to say anything," I told Ruthie.

She was sitting beside me, a schoolbag between her legs.

"That's okay," she answered. "I'll do it someday."

I wondered what Mary Jane Byrd might have said about this,
and I didn't know. I thought of my golfing pals—Arch Stewart
and Ray Berger and Coke Johnson—and I didn't know. I
thought about the twenty-six states I'd visited and the Italian
food I prefer and the lamebrain way I go about finances, and
I didn't know. And then Jimmy and Carla returned and Ruthie
stood up to shake my hand.

"Maybe Montana," she said. "Maybe that's where I'll go."

"Yes," I said. "Good luck."

And next Jimmy came back and it was time to say good-bye
to him too.

"Don't come back," I said.

Carla was in the back of the car, maybe asleep.

"You're pissed," he said.

I was practically inside him now, as close to him as that name
of mine he'd used way back when. He had dropped away from
me years ago, and now I was dropping away from him.

"I don't want to hear from you ever again, do you understand?" I had made a fist and held it under his chin, out of sight
of his family. "I weigh a hundred and ninety pounds, Jimmy
Spalding, I work every day out here with my hands, and I
expect I could really hurt you."

His eyes widened slowly, by degrees, and then he understood.

"This is sad, isn't it?" he said.

Here it was that I noticed his teeth. It was hard to tell which one had been knocked out, they were so shiny and even. He was that guy on TV who sells cars or land in Texas.

"My friend," I said, "this is downright pitiful."

. . .

In *The Music Man,* my favorite musical, we learn there is trouble in River City. There is trouble and it is fixed by brass and ooom-pah-pah and spirited marching and by what chemicals are released in the brain when folks find themselves caught up in the big parade. I had that on my mind when Jimmy left, and I set about to vacuum and dust and wipe away any evidence that he'd come through my house. I took an inventory of myself—the growing pot belly Johnny Carson laughs at, and the bad right knee Dr. Weems says he'd like to fix one day— and with the record player going loud as thunder I had my house all to myself, and feelings I believe in.

I thought of Victor Fears, who was coming to loan me money, and Janet Miller, who is a Mesilla Park jeweler I sometimes sleep with. And then, the Shirelles singing to me about how it was between boys and girls, I thought of Mary Jane Byrd—what flower she smelled like and how she could roll over in a way that made nighttime beautiful.

"Oh, Lord," I said to myself and the walls.

Maybe she would be up by now, I thought. And maybe she'd like to hear from someone—a terrible me—that she'd once known.

I would not want to be one of those memoirists who begin a recollection by saying, "Attention, people, there is a dead dog in these pages," but, alas, I am and there is. In fact, now that I puzzle it through from the higher ground of time and distance, I see not one but two dead dogs. My wife, Vicki, who is suing me for divorce and without whom I once thought it inconceivable to live, says we dare not treat our pets—the cats and dogs, even the reptiles only the odd truly love—with more irony, or indifference, than we treat ourselves. It is a truism (no more original or startling than the vast blue sky our heaven is here in southern New Mexico) that you can tell much about a person by the way he treats his animals: brutes for brutes, she once explained, lapdogs for the lovely inside. They are our analogues, these hounds. Us without the fret-filled, overlarge brain. Us would we only bound and bark and fetch when the urge strikes us.

The dog that concerns me first is the one, waterlogged and huge, I dragged from a pond in Capitan, New Mexico, over a month ago. We were staying in Lincoln, population fifty-two, a wide swerve in the road, where my father-in-law, a bronze sculptor and tyrannical zoning commission chairman, has his dream house. It was in the guest quarters out back where Vicki, level-headed as the Republican state senator she is, said we could go to repair the rot-weakened timbers that were our marriage. "We will do nothing here but sleep and eat and talk," she said, and for five days, watched over by the part-time artists and cowboys and rich folks who are my in-laws' buddies, that's exactly what we did. We hiked the one street of that town—a crumbling United States highway—from the stuccoed adobe courthouse Billy the Kid once blasted his way out of at one end, to the narrow bridgeworks the Army Corps of Engineers was putting riprap around that summer. Late enough at night to watch the deer trot down out of the mountain behind us to feast on pears and apples in the orchards (or on my mother-in-law's garden of lettuce and yellow corn), Vicki and I recognized the strangers we'd become to each other since our courting days as sophomores at the University of New Mexico. Yes, we were proud of our kids, Debbie and Bobby Phelps, Jr., and still carefree enough to try the watusi or the frug at the Mimbres Valley Country Club over in Deming, where we live (and where I sell more Chevrolets than any other car dealer in our deserts). As Christians, we were satisfied, not smug, and a bit humbled by the charitable, lofty view we took of humankind; we had all the virtues—thrift, honesty, a respect for the creature parts of us—but by the fifth day it was clear, but unspoken, that we did not have love, the one thing that was to make our lives wonderful, no matter how narrow or deprived they might otherwise be.

On the fifth day we drove the eighteen miles of switchbacks

and dangerous hills to Capitan, which is a no-account crossroads of necessary businesses—a laundry, a Piggly Wiggly market, a post office—known to the big world as the town nearest
the birthplace of Smokey the Bear (whose face, by the way, is
seen on signs and paper bags and calendars often enough to
bring out the hating half of you). "Let's play tennis," Vicki had
suggested, and so there we were, roasted by a sun you can get
damn tired of, bouncing to and fro in a chain-link–enclosed
rectangle of green concrete not ten paces from a highway
intersection a drunk could doze in fearlessly. I played this game
in a frenzy, I tell you. The sportsman in me, that nagging
wild-haired infant inside who knows only perfection and how
far short of it we are, was in high form that day. He raged at
her for being too slow. And too clumsy. He picked on her
swing, which was too fussy and full of elbow to be choice. He
begged her to pay attention, for crying out loud, and to stop
kidding around. "Oh," she scolded once, "just shut up, you!"
She threw him the finger once, and told him—that ugly loudmouth sore loser inside me—to blow it out his ear. We were
fighting, our medium an optic orange Wilson tennis ball and
two Prince racquets her daddy had made us the loan of. I tried,
I confess, to drive a serve down her throat, or catch her in the
fanny (she was laughing at my shorts, I remember, and speaking satirically about the skinny, lazy man's legs I have). "Ah-
hah," she said, hands on her hips, her cum laude chin in the
air the way it gets when an Albuquerque Democrat makes an
ass out of himself in public. "You're useless," she said. "I could
just beat the pants off you, Bobby Joe."

By the second set we had forsaken talking in favor of blasting
that ball back and forth. Grim, unhappy people, we were. This
was work, not play. Our sweat and grunts had become the wet
and sounds of average folks trying to prove the impossible by
hurling themselves, time and time again, against a wall too

high, too wide and too thick to get over or around or through. Funny thing is, while she glared and scowled, I loved her. I swatted and she flailed, and all I could wonder about—in the deeper tissues of my brain where, I believe, juice and joy are one—was how much I loved that outraged woman over there. I loved how the Dunlap's department store shorts creeped up her butt, and how she bit her lip in frustration, and the child's yip-yip noise she made charging the net. Love, the force and want of it, ripped through the center of me, leaving me to be king and clown both. There it is, I kept telling myself. And I can't have it. It has legs and good breasts and makes a loud song in bed, and I don't have it anymore. I thought to hop the net, but was hobbled by the pride in me. Longingly and wholeheartedly, I imagined myself as the sort of man, wearing a red carnation in his lapel, who appears at a woman's door with a fancy-wrapped box of Valentine candy, plus a typed sonnet of his own composition, full of faith in the fairy tale Hallmark tells us about male-female relations. I tried to apologize once, but what tumbled out, made gibberish by the stubborn grown-up I am, was only "Guh, guh, guh," which Vicki looked mindful over but finally shook away with a shrug. "Hit the ball, Bobby Joe Phelps," she ordered. She stood hundreds and hundreds and hundreds of yards away now, I believed. I let go a deep breath, one from my flat and sore feet. "Yes, ma'am," I said. Silently, I went to the service line. I had shut down inside, gone still as a ghost town; there was nothing in the flesh of me but wind and dry, cracked organs. "Ready?" I almost snarled; but when I turned around, she was spun away from me and pointing.

"Look," she was saying. Adjacent to our court was an acre of grasses and weeds and gnarled plant life that is supposed to be government's idea of the ground cover and landscape we have here in the Southwest—pigweed and nutgrass and cacti and mesquite bushes, growth that needs no water to be hearty and is a pain to yank free of your lilies or roses or other foreign flowers—each patch of it identified by a sign saying what to avoid eating and how the world might have looked hundreds of years before white men settled here. A part of this space, nearest us and big as a public putting green, was a pond, green and silly and wrong for our arid earth. "What is it?" I said, and then, as if thrown into gear again, the picture in front of me lurched and got loud. "It's *drownding,*" a woman was hollering. "It's *drownding.*" For a second I wondered what English she'd learned, and then Vicki was saying to me, "It's a dog, Bobby Joe. Over there."

A ball squeezed in one hand, too-expensive racquet in the other, I watched a dog—an important one, it turned out—thrash up and down three or four times in that pond, its struggle mostly over and futile. In the park, citizens were going whichaway in confusion, and somebody, in a too-vowely Odessa-like voice, was yelling, "I can't swim," and Vicki was telling me to run over there and pull that dog out, goddammit. I looked at my sneakers, which were Adidas and not bought for wading in muck, and waited for my thoughts to turn generous. Yonder, Vicki had her woman's fist up, tiny but capable, and was shaking it my way. "Bobby Joe," she said. Her voice was warning only. "Okay," I said, attending to the husband half of me; I had been told what to do and now, reluctantly and stupidly, I was doing it.

·   ·   ·

I hated that dog I wrestled out of that scummy water—hated it for the dumb, hairy thing it was to have panicked and to have gone down and down and down; hated it for its awkward weight and sloppy jaws and useless limp legs; hated it because

I was soaked and it was already dead and because my wife, usually sensible as a banker, was the first among the half-dozen on the slippery bank where I dropped the animal to insist I push on its chest, under the ribs, respirate it or resuscitate it or just do some damn thing. "Jesus, Vicki," I said. "It's too late, all right?" It lay beside me, a collarless mongrel that might have been half wild in the first place, red and black, the product of years and years of just hunching and eating and sleeping full at night. "Just try," she said, "it's better than nothing." I studied her and it, my wife and the thing she was currently rooting for. I thought about the constellations sometimes seen hereabouts—Andromeda, Cepheus, Cassiopeia; I thought, seriously and too long, about our hometown pals—Walt Scoggins, J.B. and Bonnie Streeter, old Bucky Waters—and the life-affirming Labor Day bar-b-que we throw. A man stood next to Vicki, and I remember thinking how nifty his Stetson-like cowboy hat was and how, were I a less domestic man, I'd like to buy it and soon enough swagger into a saloon for a shot of Wild West red-eye. "Five minutes," I told her. "I'll do it for five minutes."

Hardly a minute later she shoved me aside, forced all forty-one of her years into my shoulder and told me to move the hell out of the way. "You coward," she snapped. In her voice was the farm girl and rodeo queen and double-A basketball forward she'd once been. "He was doing it all wrong," she said; and I saw the woman for whom the dog was *drownding* nod and make a face I could not take the measure of. Vicki was amazing, she was. Straddling that dog, she pushed the heels of her hands under its ribcage. She called that dog a low-down bastard and used other language I'd once heard her throw a Sinclair Oil lobbyist out of her office with; deep in me, it was comforting to think that the dog, from its black hereafter, might be reached with such talk and thus come howling back into the here-and-now. "Come on, dog," she said. "Don't you dare quit on me." I felt like a stranger now, no more related to this drama than I am to those catastrophes we hear about from China. I was here, all mostly good six feet of me; and she was there, on her knees, in the mud. I was in a car going hither or in a plane bound for the make-believe outlands of Timbuktu; and she, a woman with a familiar name and a laugh I used to know in darkness, was in a different place and time, me merely a dumbbell to read about one day.

And then it was over. A cloud had gone by, changed shapes a dozen times, and was now a milky streak at the horizon. "What?" I said. She was standing near me, her expression empty space that could not be read into or be made warmly human. I was going to learn something, I knew. Working on that dog, trying to put its magic back, she had come to a decision about us. The dog, the stink and bulk of him, was a 3-D thing she'd spent time and feeling on, and now she had come to me again, another beast that was maybe already gone to her. I could smell me, I remember. Part English Leather my daughter, Debbie, had given me for Christmas, part athletics, part pond water. Watching Vicki, I recalled some things I knew: my first fistfight, the warped dreams I often shake from, how money feels in my wallet. My arm had an itch I would not scratch; my brain a need I could not act on. Everything hereabouts—these average citizens, that scraggly cottonwood, this infernal air we breathe—was both itself and not, and it was simple to believe that what held me here on earth was cheap, weak and loose.

"You want me to go," I said. Her head went *yes* a little and I could feel the separate, common strings of me pop free. "Where?" I asked. Immediately, I saw how things would be henceforth: the Triangle Drive-In, where I eat chicken-fried steak and bullshit with Del Cruz, the five-bedroom home I only drive by now, the remote-control TV I watch too much of in the duplex I rent on Olive Street. "Go away, Bobby Joe," Vicki said. "I don't care where."

So I did.

.   .   .

The other dog that died was named Gigi Babette Regis III, a black registered toy poodle, its mother Babette Coco Village, its father Regis Antoine Pierre II; and that fine dog—which was called Sheri—had papers that went back to the days when Indians fought palefaces and travel by steamship was a big damn deal. An ordinary house pet, it was—in the innocent years long before Vicki and I flew apart one month ago—her dog and, sad to say, I actually killed it.

Coming home from work one night, after drinking Jack Daniel's that was no good for me and after making calls to women I had no right to know or to bother, I pulled into my driveway and felt a bump that, I hoped then, could not have been live or meaningful. It was dark on that side of the house and I remember saying to myself, "Bobby, you ought to put the car in the garage." On the radio was the music I buy, what is sung about in Houston and Nashville, unashamed and from the heart of things. This was 1975, when our news concerned Jim "Catfish" Hunter and hoodlums named Mitchell and Haldeman and John D. Erlichman, and I owned a half-million dollars of shiny inventory the better businessmen at Honda and Datsun aimed to make me swallow whole. I sat in my driveway for a time, muttering, "Shit, shit, shit," and then, careful as any drunk, I eased my Impala into the garage. Things will get better, I told myself.

At first, I tried to ignore the black lump her dead dog was. I watched Marvin Stapleton's house across the way and noted the banging coming from his garage. In the east, the moon was partly up, shining down on the sixty barren flat miles between me and another town of workaday folks. I remembered the bit of dirty Spanish I knew and the faraway countries of Persia and France I intended to visit. That dog was Vicki's practically all its life. She had raised it, taught it the customary tricks—to sit and to heel, to roll over and to beg—and now there would be nothing to sleep in the curl of her in our big bed. Hell, I liked it too, that silly poodle. It came when called, did its business outdoors as it ought. It liked to ride on my lap and chase whatever I tossed. In its way, it was as steadfast a pal as any human I'd known as long. Truth to tell, though from a breed often vain as the royalty I've read about, that dog probably thought of itself as a mutt, not as twenty-five pounds of muscle worth over five hundred dollars to folks with breeding kennels.

Vicki took it well, I thought. She switched off the shoot-'em-up Karl Malden was starring in and looked at me squarely, nothing in her eyes about the cross-hearted, angry thing this should have been. "Tell me that again, Bobby," she said. I'd seen her look before, but for a moment I couldn't place it. "Say it again, Bobby." I heard the children in the living room, Bobby Jr. trying to learn what nine times x was and Debbie being helpful with advice about integers. I took in the character of my rec room, the two golf trophies I'd won and the nine-point buck I'd bow-shot one winter in the Gila Forest. It was this way, I told her. It was dark, I was indecisive and maybe not concentrating as one should, and well, it was a mistake. "An accident," she said. Her hand went through her hair twice, and instantly I recognized her expression. I'd seen it the summer before when, near the shallow end of the club pool, I'd confessed to sleeping with my accountant, Mildred Tanner. Against the sun, she'd shaded her eyes and said, quietly,

"Bobby, you're a stupid man." Now, she lighted a menthol cigarette, and the present came rushing back.

"Tell me again, Bobby. Slowly, this time." A cloud of smoke came my way, and I realized I was frightened. This is fury, I told myself. This is rage without the volume and lashing out. "What do you want to know?" I asked. She used silence the way actors do, knowing it had weight and color and shape. Then: "What were you thinking of, tell me that." I heard myself again: how I'd been at the Thunderbird Lounge with Jimmy Stokes and the Clute brothers; how, between jokes and drinks, we'd fixed the world and pitched ourselves high up on the heap we saw. I'd listened to Uncle Roy and the Red Creek Wranglers, I told her, and was especially impressed by the wild notes they reached. I re-created my wandering ride home, up Fir Street and down Iron, onto I-10 for twenty miles of trucks roaring past. "I want to know what was on your mind," she said. "I want to know what sort of person you are." I was thinking about shoes then, I said, how new ones are a pleasure and yet polishing a chore. I had thought about running, which I was once fair at, and how much I hated the paperwork that buying and selling are. And then, while my house made mechanical noises and something jetlike could be heard flying far overhead, it was her turn.

"This is what you'll do," she said. This was it, she was really saying. I was not to disappoint, or hurt, her again. I was to shave every morning, including weekends. I was to get my hair cut twice a month. I was to stop cussing. I was to cast aside my affection for bombing America's enemies. "Go to the linen closet," she said, "and get out one of the monogrammed bath towels. Put the dog in the towel, and in the backyard, by the upright willow, dig a hole." Were I to fail her again, she was saying, in a month or a year or even ten years, I was finished. There was no such thing as accident. There was only us and the busy world itself. There was only her and me, and events that were the true expression of us. No bad luck. No misfortune. No happenstance. Just the sad character I was and the grief I left behind me. "Tell me," she actually said, "when you're done."

. . .

What do I see, now that this story has moved sufficiently backward? I see a man whose favorite food was spaghetti and whose happiest color was the yellow you find on certain doctors and dentists at the golf course. I see him—this man I am related to only by time and specific memories—at work in his backyard around midnight, his ordinary world asleep and tending toward dreamland. But what can be done to express his state of mind? It's like watching home movies. You know the names of these folks—Uncle Boots, your granny, that toddler who is the fat, grinning image of you—but you do not know, though you think you do, the secret insides of them. They are only light and shadow, sound and movement; then they are vanished.

My jacket folded over one willow limb, I dug a proper hole in the hour I was outside alone. I kept my thoughts to the work I did in the place I was: the dirt, the shovel, the ache in my spine, the blisters that would appear in the morning. Then I knocked on the window to tell Vicki to come out. She was beautiful, I remember, all leg and arm and heroine's shiny hair; and I did well to resist the desire to grab her and hold on. "I'm sorry," I said. She looked at me as if I were a guy she'd bumped fenders with at the supermarket. "It's kind of cold, isn't it, Bobby?" This was only polite talk; it wasn't nighttime in March she was thinking of. "You want to say something?" she asked. "It is a burial, after all." She stood next to the hole,

staring down at the towel and the lump underneath, and I
could think of no words to explain that and me both. "Go over
there a minute, Bobby," she said. I saw her slippers and the
blue robe that was a birthday gift, and as if I had a real weight
to drag, I went some paces away. Once upon a time, she was
an expert dancer, able to throw herself heedlessly into the steps
we knew. She could play bridge too. And knit well enough to
give her handiwork as presents. I'd seen her ride her daddy's
meanest horse, a gelding named Scooter, and slug it when it
misbehaved. I remembered her favorite books and the French
history she liked to study, and then, in what was the climax of
this night, she came toward me and said all right, I could cover
the hole now. "Be sure to clean up before you go inside," she
said. "Mrs. Tipton waxed the floors today."

She was asleep when I came in. I put on my pajamas, and
when I lay down, I was surprised that the world didn't tilt
more. Our house was silent, Vicki was mostly still, and I was
wondering about the jobs I'd accomplish by noon. This, I see
now, was the true end of us; there would be only years and one
more dead dog to make it plain for me. But this night, my clock
radio showing how late it was, I was counting the employees
I had, thirty-one, and visualizing the new showroom I was
building, and telling myself that everything—Vicki, our children, me—was all right. I was happy, I told myself. Lord, I was
very, very happy.

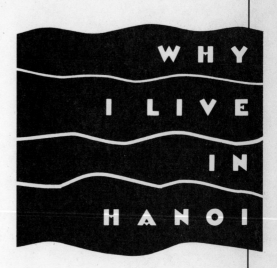

WHY
I LIVE
IN
HANOI

Uncle Sugar asked me why I crapped out, deserted. To be true, it wasn't political or high-minded. Mr. Charles wasn't special to me. Far as I knew he was cruelty and sin, just like the brass said. "Ape and leech," Captain Blood said to me one time. This was a month before I split. "That's your average Cong. Now, your French-speaking hostile, he's a different story." Indeed, it wasn't Charles or morality or weakness of spirit. It was fear.

Fear started the day I hit Soc Trang and met Blood. The heat was like a screaming fat lady sitting on your neck, and Sock Trang was all misery and CS gas, with only one permanent building, and an OP shack of corrugated tin.

"This is home, Walker," Blood said. "We got all the comforts here. We got Mother's cooking, direct communication with the World, superior company and unfriendly neighbors."

"That's fine," I said. I told him I was high school educated, courteous, just had the misfortune of being poor and living close to the draft board. I was nervous, aiming to please.

Then he wanted to know if I was testicular.

"That's me," I said.

"That's balls, Walker," he barked. He was looking at his shoes—snakeskin and Imported, definitely not Issue. "We're H and I here, Tump. Hit and Interdict. We're courageous and full of good feelings."

"Yes, sir," I said. "Me too."

Blood was from Arkansas and there was weight in his voice. Plus, he had a wing-tip nose like a big man's shoe.

"We're here," he was saying, "and we're right. I'm a moral man, Tump. Married and a proud father, et cetera. I make friends easily, am loyal, and write regular. I am good to my people. I bring in entertainment and happiness too. You got to live up to my standards."

"I'm the same," I said. I told him I was from Brownfield, Texas and not ashamed of anything. "My nose is clean," I said, "and I am going home heroic and a credit to my family." I was eighteen, you got to remember, and pompous. Besides, this was 1968 and these sentiments seemed proper.

"Also," Blood said, "you got to be a banzai criminal Arab gangbuster."

I could be that too, I said. I had anecdotes ready in case he asked, youth stuff and escapades.

"I want loconess on my side." Blood was looking at a big contour map of Vietnam MR2 on the wall, and pointing. "You know what that is?"

Soc Trang looked meager and sissy up against swamp and numbered hills.

"That's craziness," I said.

I had taken a chance, relying on native guile and luck.

"You do okay, Tump Walker, and I'll make you one grand

pussy warrior." Then he smiled like a daddy and I was drowned with relief.

Within the hour I was making friends, all like myself— common and bound by hard luck. I was moved in with Texans, the theory being that we had a tradition of manhood and frontier thinking to uphold. Right away I met Sandman, from Big Spring. He was asleep and snoring like a bandsaw, dreaming (I learned later) of cowpokes and innocence. There was also a Hawaiian who called himself LBJ and said he was all shit-kicker underneath. And a couple of others: San Antonio Mexicans named Cisco and Pancho, both in black-market sombreros. They were skinny—all breath and britches—and short-timers, soon to go home.

Last was best.

"Go on, white boy," he said. "Ask my name."

He was black, wearing a steel pot so you could see nothing but white eye movement and pink tongue.

"Name's Poetry," he said, laughing. " 'Cause I'm always in motion. "You can call me P."

Then he showed me his Sixteen.

"This is my sonnet," he said, adding that bullets were a high form of versification, like 'palm and Elephant Feet and MACV phosphorous guns. P had College written all over him: "A and M basketball. I was into metaphysics and high expectations," he said. We were eating cling peaches and pressed meat. "Mr. Charles," P said, "has a deep appreciation for light verse."

I said I'd heard that. I was lying. Fear, again.

"Ask me how I know that's true," he said.

I did, and P told about the time Captain Blood took the Texans into a village in the Ir Drang Valley. "That night," Poetry said, "everybody got dressed up in tiger suits, night-fighter cosmetic and Jade East, creeped up an irrigation ditch, and then went in singing ballads and Holy Roller hymns."

"Charles was humiliated," LBJ said. "And slayed."

Poetry was giggling. "Place was full of James Brown tapes and pamphlets about love."

"LBJ had a hard-on for a week," Cisco said.

The Hawaiian had a face full of embarrassment. Apparently, he was a mean monkey, made horny and deadly by love.

"It was real mortal," Poetry announced finally. He was serious. He'd be dead in a month, and I'd be here, in Happy Hanoi, in two. Little did I know, etc.

As soon as the sun went down, I started writing the President and kept at it for many weeks, getting a letter off every day. "You sent me to Mars," I scribbled. I was simple-minded and hateless, I told him, a former Bulldog infielder and a lover of auto mechanics. I told him I was in the company of ding-dongs and inefficiency. There were Muslims here and three guys, San Francisco vegetarians, calling themselves the Cult of the Damned. "Mr. President," I wrote, "I only want to go home, work in my Daddy's Texaco station and maybe screw around a bit before I get serious and begin my career." I told him we got rain every night. *Rain* was Vietnam for "Incoming Rounds." "Incoming" was Charles for *woe* and *hurt feelings* (my italics).

Then I got a letter. From my daddy.

"What say, John Wayne?" "John Wayne" was Poetry for yours damn truly. It was mockery.

I ripped into that letter and was immediately crestfallen.

"Tump, you jerk," was how it started. My daddy was letting me know how disappointed he was. "You candy-ass," he wrote, saying that the FBI had come round to see him. "They disapproved. They said President Johnson disapproved. They said that if you ever wrote again, they'd break my legs and blind your Momma."

That afternoon Blood made a speech. He was bringing starlets in the next day and wanted us to be in the mood. This was

at mess call, us gobbling up Mother's chop. Mother was a
sawed-off Cincinnati hood with eyes full of amphetamine fuzz.

"I got a big heart," Blood was saying.

It was furnace hot, naked being the dress of the day, but
everybody was soldier-ready and hard-core, so Blood got our full
attention. There was ROTC skill and in every word authority.
For twenty minutes he addressed themes of mutual impor-
tance—toil and cleanliness and etiquette. It was inspirational.
I was thinking of home—those amber waves of grain, that
purple mountain thing.

"I want to end on a note of triumph," Blood said. "But I
can't. I keep thinking about scum-suckers and layabouts."

This was sad. I felt he was talking about me.

"I got nigger tight-end Razorback stories like you wouldn't
believe," he said. "I got farm stories and traveling-salesmen
jokes and first-love heartbreakers. I got stories about tactics and
surviving on rabbit and toad. But I keep returning to despair."

By this time everybody was crying, the guy next to me—a
Montana medic named Nightingale—honking up buggers and
intestinal rot.

"Yes, sir," Blood said, his voice rising with conviction. "I
keep thinking about them." He was pointing to the jungle
beyond our cleared perimeter.

Everyone looked out, tense. I felt a chill go through me, my
breath like water. Blood was right. You could tell the woods
were full of hopelessness.

It was a genuine, testicular moment.

· · ·

That night we got *rain* and a lecture by Mr. Charles. Poetry
said Charles had a bullhorn and a comic-book command of
English. "His name's Tong," Poetry said. I learned, by way of

biography, that Tong was French (he said), thereby sensitive and more theoretical than cutthroat.

"Good morning, bloodthirsty GI."

Looking out, you could see nothing but different degrees of two-A.M. darkness.

"You got homesickness, GI, Charles knows. Land of plenty, Social Security and all that jazz."

"That's ideology," P said, pulling his poncho over his head and rolling into a corner of our hooch.

Cisco and Pancho were pissed. They took these nightly lectures personally.

Charles said he knew all this stuff 'cause he infiltrated. He was a bad-ass dude, cunning and savage. Charles said he was invincible, a myth. "Ask *New York Times*," he said. "They myth, too." Later he played Beach Boy records and read captured mail.

"PFC Roberto Muniz," Tong said. "I hold picture here of chick like nasty dream."

Muniz was an Ohio spic. This news went to his heart like an ice pick and you could hear him yowl for an hour.

"Oooopppss," said Tong, "bad news for Donnie T. Bobo."

Bobo was a Floridian, idleness his strong suit.

"Capitalist repossess customized Buick and way of life. Ruling class rob you of wheels and innocence. Too bad."

Then Tong hit close to home: me.

"Ah, Tump Walker. I hold letter from Baptist preacher. Say you must buck up, not be panty-waist."

About then I started crying. Gut sobs, you know, ruptures. Here I was, I said to myself, just stupid, silly-shit me. All the Texans were sleeping, except Cisco and Pancho. What am I doing here, I wondered. I asked all the raggedy-assed questions: about virtue and such. This introspection went on for a half-hour before I hit dreamland.

. . . .

I tried to go AWOL when the Osmonds died. The Osmonds were Utah Mormons, in the war for pride and tests of faith. Charles hit us with a shitstorm, an hour of murder and saddened lives. Poetry went crazy with vengeance, his Sixteen on auto, pouring yellow pee-fire into the darkness. Sandman woke up and hurled cuss words, inventive Big Spring colloquialisms about quote cattle and windy days unquote. Cisco and Pancho moaned while bullets shredded green cover and thudded into bunkers. Then there was this boom and a sudden vacuum of quiet and anticipation.

"Bad news," P said.

LBJ agreed, in Hawaiian.

A moment later the sound came in a like a tidal wave, wounds and screams riding its crest. You knew then that the Osmonds had fried. At dawn, you could see the wreckage and mourning. Their hooch, the Tabernacle, was flattened, ground zero, no-account fires burning at the edges. The Osmonds had already been removed.

"This is the kind of thing you remember," Blood said by way of consolation. "It tends to make you hardheaded and mean."

Consequently, all us desperadoes were numb with grief when the starlets arrived.

"Ahhh, perk up, you party-poopers," said one.

It was afternoon and they were doing a show to lift our spirits, courtesy of the USO and friends in high places. The one talking was Debbi, Louisiana bred with a loaf of moss in her voice. She'd been in two Italian westerns, in each a blonde with an epic body. She was special, you could tell.

"Why, you all are just a bunch of wet blankets." Her hands were on her hips in real disapproval, looking over the fifty of us—we Texans in front—tsking and wagging the naughty finger. She was peeved.

"Me and my friends," she was saying, "we come all this way—hot, sacrificing, riding in second-class transport—"

It was then LBJ went obscene.

"Show us your humpers!" he shouted. All the carnage had made him hot to trot.

"Well, that's more like it." She brightened immediately. "Girls," she called, and from Captain Blood's OP shack came a herd of starlets in bathing suits and sex. As a result, wildness seized us all.

"Oh, Cisco!" Pancho had risen as if moved by a particularly deep terror.

Cisco was pawing the ground and rocking forward: "Oh, Pancho!"

That was all it took. Crazy with beauty and death, we set upon them. You could hear the roars for miles, I'm sure: pig-grunting and squeals of conquest. Once I looked up and saw Poetry sucking a starlet's ankle. She was delighted. One beauty had six grunts on her, Nightingale nursing at her nips. Bobo was there too, his eyes rolled into his head in ecstasy. OD'd on narcotics and Hollywood gossip. For my part, I felt empty, weak and afraid. There was disorder all around. Mother, the cook and hood, was wailing on a Cornhusker who'd interfered. Dust boiled up and security, I'm sure, was forgotten. Then I saw Blood, smirking over his achievement: he'd turned us away from grief and into healthier emotions.

I caught Debbi when the starlets were saying bye-bye, their choppers having set down in the LZ and trembling like grasshoppers.

"Take me with you," I said.

Her face was dark with confusion.

"Me," I said. "I want to go." What with tears on my cheeks
and shirt open for comfort, I was a sight and a surprise. "I'll
pay," I said, pulling out my pockets. The chopper was getting
ready to leave and, sad to say, she wanted her hand. Her friends
were trying to help her out, one of them—a Bostonian, I
believe—kicking at my shins.

"I love you," I said. "I love everybody."

She appealed to my patriotism.

I shook my head.

"Asshole," she said.

Her pals were dragging her into the chopper. I wouldn't let
go. That Bostonian was working me over good, pulling my hair
and whipping me with her belt.

The chopper shivered and started to lift, the howl of the
rotors above my yells. Debbi's face was full of disgust. "You
crumb," she hollered. "Let go!"

I wouldn't. Slowly the chopper rose, wobbling, starlets spilling from the webbed seats inside, girlish eeks filling the air. I
was starting to lose my grip.

"Bite him," ordered that Bostonian. She was truly offended.
A makeup bag thudded against my head. Then Debbi's teeth
came out and she went for my hand. You could hear the flight
officer pumping the rotor pedals, blades whirring and screeching, that chopper rocking twenty meters in the air. I was trying
to grab hold of the runners and yelling about what a gentleman
I was and how I'd work for free. I told them I'd take them all
to Texas. We'd party, I said, and be noisy. But it was too late.
Debbi was working seriously on one finger.

"Okay," I said, pulling my hand free and falling in a heap.

From then on I wasn't the same.

. . . .

Blood was mortified, his face red with shame. "Ah, Tump," he said wistfully. We were sitting in the OP shack, all the Texans scowling at me. There was tension and recrimination in the air. Obviously I had let them down; I'd been a spectacle. P particularly seemed repulsed, his eyes hooded and inhuman. It was fear, I wanted to say. Nothing personal, I liked them all.

"I got a mission," Blood was saying. "Gonna teach you manners and courage." You could tell he was heartbroken. "Y'all in for privilege and honor." He hung fire, laughing to himself. "Y'all is gonna get Mr. Tong."

We left at midnight, the six of us in camouflage, looking like animals and indigenous flora. Poetry was in charge and made me take point.

"It's a poise test," P said. "You just watch me. I dance, you dance. I fart, you fart. Life is easy, John Wayne, and Poetry is poise."

He gave me a shove and off I stumbled, an ocean of sweat already rolling off my breastbone. As we split, you could hear the slope combo Captain Blood had brought in for the occasion. The combo was Dr. Filth and the Leather Cup, the Doctor a squatty sort and mysterious. When we hit the jungle, the Cup was singing about deceit, high hopes, and the fools that lovers be.

For the first hour, nothing happened. No Tong, no Dinks, just darkness and everlasting gloom. I tippy-toed ahead, wincing with each cracked twig and crushed leaf. I felt clumsy and stupid peering into that blackness, my Sixteen lead-heavy and cold. After a while, the moon came out, its light dripping off the branches like milk. I didn't know where we were, but every now and then you'd catch—when the wind was right, I suppose—a note or two from Dr. Filth. He'd be singing about high-heeled sneakers and shaking that money-maker, drums thundering and guitars crashing.

Once I thought I saw something, and went scurrying back.

"Up there," I said, pointing wildly. "I saw one. Black jamies, the works."

Poetry looked skeptical. I tried to be convincing.

"He had a scar," I said, "on one cheek. He looked experienced too, like he'd been out here for years. He was short, a runt probably."

I went on like this for five minutes, explaining how he moved (like a cat) and how I saw him leaning against a tree like he was just another person on a busy street. I was hopped up when I finished, and breathless. "It was a Zip, all right," I said.

Poetry was unimpressed. "John Wayne," he said, "you a shame to yo' momma and Uncle Sugar both."

Then he gave me a kick in the can and I drag-assed back to point feeling embarrassed and woebegone.

I don't know what time it was when Mr. Tong came on the air with his propaganda and psywar. We were on a piss break, the Texans strung out in a line, me hanging on like an afterthought. I was cramped up with fear.

"Good morning, American Running Dogs!"

Instantly we were a maze of mob movement, scrambling and diving and scooting in a frenzy. It sounded like Tong was right above us, his bullhorn squealing from the dark canopy of jungle over our heads.

LBJ was for shaking trees and random fire.

Cisco and Pancho were huddled at the base of a cao-dai tree, sneering and muttering dirty Spanish.

Sandman was spitting Texas local color, a twisted whispered paragraph about quote ripping off his arms and beating him with the mangled stumps unquote.

Poetry had a better idea. "Surprise," he said.

I was for withdrawing or lying low.

"Wrong," P said, fixing me with a hard, evil look. "You go

thataway and we'll go thisaway." In a second they vamoosed, seemingly melting into the foliage, and I was scuttling belly-down along the ground, trying almost to pull it over me.

Except for Tong, it was quiet, the Leather Cup having quit in mid-lyric. I imagined everybody back at Soc Trang, hopping and smoking reefer, and then Tong's outburst, and everybody freezing, Dr. Filth's jaw open and unable to complete a sentiment about boys and girls and backseat romance; and everybody—Blood included—paralyzed, eyes wide and suspicious, ears cocked for more jungle bungle.

Tong was unfazed, a squawking chatterbox of promises and achievements.

Movement was scary. I felt namelessnesses crawling on me—fire ants, probably, and decaying crud. The moon shone fiercely now, shapes leaping up from every corner. One second there'd be nothing; the next, a Cong tank cranking and grinding toward my chest.

"No, no, no," I said to myself. "I ain't scared. I'm a banzai criminal Arab gangbuster." It was self-deception.

There was another burst of fire, sounding toylike but nearby.

Mr. Charles, Tong, seemed somewhere off to my right, floating like a ghost. He was upset, you could tell, upbraiding us Yankees for crimes and poor behavior.

Heart thumping in my throat, I found a likely bush and hugged it, discovering I was on the edge of a clearing about the size of a rich man's living room. Across the way you could see muzzle flashes and occasionally the moonlit figure of a foundering Texan.

I waved, but they didn't notice. I tried yelling, but no words came out, there being dust inside me and hard, continuous winds.

The moon was a spotlight shining on this enterprise alone. Tong was up there, fifteen or twenty meters above me, I knew it. It seemed I could hear his breath, strong and unlabored; I could feel him shifting position on his perch, and knew his brain as if it were my own.

"Remember the Alamo!" somebody was yelling.

The Texans were maneuvering, darting from tree to tree, LBJ bellyflopping into a nest of vines and leafy rot. They were taking return fire from somewhere, branches exploding all around, ricochets zinging, the air around my ears going whump-whump-whump. The smell was of gunpowder and disturbed earth and the gruesome human desire.

It was then I heard some Hanoi chittering. To my right— seen only by me, I now believe—hunkered two Charleses, one of them scar-faced and familiar. He was the Hostile from before. I *had* seen him! The air went out of me in a rush. I hadn't seen a hallucination or a vision.

He and his buddy were firing from behind a fallen log, the ground around them burning like white powder, bone-light.

From the Texans I could hear whimpering, awful dog noises from a fully grown man. Somebody'd been hit and was failing bravery.

"Git some! Git some!" That was Poetry, being encouraging and fearless.

When I brought my Sixteen up, I could smell myself. I was sweating fish grease, drenched and clammy, on the verge of pissing my pants. I'm sure that if I could've looked into my own mouth, I would've seen my teeth glowing and rattling, a blaze of static snapping like sparks from tonsil to tonsil across my tongue.

As blank-faced as two china dolls, the Cong were busy laying down pee-fire and havoc.

"Oh, shit!" a Texan hollered with disgust. "My arm, my fucking arm!" It was Sandman, hit; I imagined him trying to punch the pain out of his bloody arm, his eyes going yellow and weak.

Above me, above us all, Tong was still carrying on about victory, self-denial and his famous national destiny. I was sick, my stomach swelling, and farting. Cutting through it all was the voice of Poetry.

"John Wayne!" he was hollering. "Help us, John Wayne!"

It was a crazy shout, like he expected Good Guys to come thundering to his aid from movieland. In his voice I could hear hopelessness and shattered nerves. You could tell then that he'd lost his good humor and his poise.

Dry-mouthed, I sprang into an Army crouch of alertness, Sixteen at my shoulder. I could feel the adrenaline kick in. It was like being bit by a Doberman guard dog. My face hurt from concentrating; and it seemed my bones were torquing, rubbing against ligament and gristle.

"John Wayne!"

For a second the two Cong were dancing, bobbing and ducking, but it was only me, struggling to sight down the barrel. The jungle was throbbing, the ground trembling and threatening to drop away beneath me. Tong was calm and trouble-free, and the Texans were crashing in the undergrowth, and ahead ten clicks or so sat the source of death and ruined futures.

Then I let go. I squeezed that trigger, hanging onto that trigger really, riding that trigger, putting it to them in a long indiscreet burst. There was only noise then, one steady rip of riflery. And me too. I was screaming: animalistic growls and yips and mean barks, etc. The bullets seemed to chew up the light, throwing it off in chunks that made me dizzy to watch. I was exhilarated and gloriously frightened, crying and laughing at the same time. Dumb as snot. Crazy thoughts tore through me: there was Debbi and Blood and my pop crippled and Poetry disappearing in a tornado of motion.

Then it was over and I found I had crapped my pants.

.   .   .

For a time I was a hero, praised and fussed over. Blood made everybody congratulate me. He said I'd greased ten Cong and liberated two Friendlies, even put me in for a citation. Mother gave me hot chow. I had my buddies back, it appeared, and life would again be easy and charming. Then Poetry died.

He got wasted by a Vespa motor scooter.

Here's what happened:

As a reward for being valiant, etc., Blood sent us Texans (all except Sandman, who'd been E-vacked by the medicos, suffering from wounds and high fever) into Gon City for rest and hellraising. We choppered out with Dr. Filth and his Cup, the five of them sick-looking in Beatle boots and Jap sportshirts. They all turned out to be ARVN grunts, regular soldiers on special assignment. Except Filth. He was brass or royalty or cocaine gangster, nobody could figure out which.

"You American GIs all number-one killer types, okay?" Filth said.

Poetry took a shine to him immediately. "Indeed and so true," he said. "We good, but John Wayne is best." He was squeezing my shoulder.

We hit Gon City red-eyed and eager.

"You come my place, get funky and down," Filth said. "I got many sex kittens and atmosphere."

LBJ went surly. He was for stomping civilians and working out his frustrations.

Cisco and Pancho were already shit-faced, blasted on dynamite made from Nightingale's morphine, rubbing alcohol, and Vitalis. They were going home soon and entitled to celebrate.

"What say, John Wayne?"

"Okey-dokey," I said, and in twenty minutes we were there—the war a million miles away, a fairy tale happening to the Other Guy.

Filth's place was essentially a tit bar—venal and very stimulating. Girls were everywhere, smiling and pretty enough to make your heart spin on a point. This was at noon. By 1730 hours, they all looked like gurus or iguanas. The chick I was sitting with was named Ming. I called her Lucy after my girl back home. This Lucy knew about a dozen words of English, mainly "Get married?," "Home of Free" and "Dingleberry."

Soon enough I was drunk and ready to leave.

"No, no," said Lucy Ming, plucking at my arm. "You like roll in grass? Hamburger with works?"

The Texans were in high spirits, Cisco and Pancho doing imitations of states of mind, including Triumph and Irony.

"Ain't this first-rate?" LBJ said. He had one B-girl in a headlock and another with her arm wrenched up her back. He was in heaven.

On the tiny dance floor Poetry was doing inspired spade moves, scooting and sliding effortlessly, his blue-black face a glaze of happiness. He dipped over my way and yelled above the band: "C'mon, boy. Move. Get up. Tomorrow it's back to evil and digging holes." For some reason I was in no mood. Onstage, Filth and his troopers were working hard, the five of them in sequins and velveteen pants, whanging away. Filth, particularly, was a powerhouse, his screeching monkey-voice hacking through a country-western tune about family troubles and Jesus Christ. To me, it was like a firefight—smoke and sweat and brain-rattling noise.

It was here the fisticuffs started.

LBJ said later it began 'cause Poetry wanted to get onstage and do Otis Redding numbers. Filth resisted; Poetry insisted.

In seconds all was turmoil and flying bottles.

Immediately I was in pain. There was a girl on the floor, coiled around my feet, biting my calf and pounding on my thigh. It was Lucy. "Hey!" I said. She looked up. "Dingle-berry." There was nothing in her eyes but determination and Oriental glee. "Stoppee," I said. I didn't know any Viet-namese. She shook her head. "Please," I said.

Poetry shot by. He had Filth by the hair, a great shining mane of it. Two of the Cup (the ones who did the doo-wahs) were whomping Poetry on the neck.

"Hit her!" he shouted.

I was confused. "She's a girl."

One of the Cup rolled against my table. Cisco, a garter belt clipped to his ears, leaped on the man's chest.

"She don't know that," Poetry was saying. "Slug her."

So I did, catching her behind the ear. Her head rang, I swear, and then very slowly the grit settled out of her face and she fell away with a thud. "Sorry," I said. I felt good then, frenzied and a hero for sure.

It was an epic fight, with lots of good-natured slugging, like in a western. For a second I felt I was home, in the Patio Bar or the El Corral, roughhousing and growing tall. Next to the bar I could see LBJ squirming through a forest of ladies' legs. A mob of B-girls was beating on his kidneys with spiked shoes, a couple of them shouting commie phrases of inspiration about throwing off the yoke, etc. Then I started laughing—a breath-less, intense and painful laughter that wasn't funny at all. Here we were, I was thinking, thumping on what Captain Blood would call our hosts and allies. It was lunatic. The place was a zoo. Charles didn't have to worry. We'd whip ourselves.

"Oh, Cisco!" Pancho had the bass-playing Cup on him, sequins coming off in a clattering shower.

Nearby Cisco exploded from a cloud of fists and swinging legs, fierce B-girls hanging from his shoulders: "Oh, Pancho!"

I was still laughing when Filth zonked me. On the way to the floor, I remember seeing Poetry, his shirt ripped, on that picayune bandstand, fending them off with a snare drum and a complex routine of kung-fu footwork. Then the lights went out.

We all came to in an alley, nobody knew where.

LBJ said it was suck city. He was for destruction.

"Calm, my son," P said. There was a pulpy knot the size of an orange on his forehead. Nearby Cisco and Pancho were a tangle of arms and legs. My head was spinning from the hurt and excitement, and my lips felt split open.

Poetry looked at me. One of his teeth was missing. It was just the ooze and flap of life, he said. He was being, of course, poetic.

After groans and moans, we were moving, arguing left or right, backward or forward. We Texans were lost, and Gon City was fearsome in the dark. A single light was burning at the corner some distance away. Stealth was rampant, it seemed, the narrow streets deserted and spooky, houses and doorways jammed up close like packing crates.

"We need direction," I said.

"You right there, John Wayne."

It seemed we were in the woods again, beyond the razor wire and bangalores, and I expected to hear Tong come on the air, squawking over his bullhorn and making our lives horrible.

Poetry heard it first, the putt-putt-putt of a scooter faint but growing louder.

"Roy Rogers," Poetry said, grinning.

Cisco and Pancho wanted to gut-shoot him, set an example.

"I'll get his attention." P stood in the middle of the muddy street, his face the picture of anticipation. It was a long wait, the rest of us leaning against a wall, listening. You could hear the thing clearly, sputtering and coughing.

"He ain't coming," LBJ said, dejected.

"Fuck if he ain't," P said. As on the first day, all I could see of him was liquid eye movement and a picket fence of teeth. "He's Roy Rogers, buckaroo and friend to lost Good Guys. He's gonna come right up here." P pointed to a spot between his feet. "He's gonna tell us where we are and where we wanna go. He don't do that, then I'm gonna stomp the yellow out of him."

The instant Roy Rogers came around that half-lit corner, he was eight parts emotion. Astonishment, mostly, and then alarm. He eyeballed the problem right away: narrow street—alley, actually—big spade in the middle hopping to and fro, doing A & M cheers of Victory.

"Whoa, boy!" Poetry was hollering.

Mr. Roy shook his head crazily. One arm thrashed the air as if trying to wave Poetry away. Roy was wailing too, his mouth eating at the air in genuine panic.

We all stopped laughing when we saw what was going to happen.

"Well, fuck me," Poetry said, seeing it too.

Then Mr. Roy hit him, that Vespa motorbike slamming into P's gut, flattening him. The sound was enormous, as if there were no other in the world but that bone-crunching thump and whoosh of breath. You could almost hear Poetry's insides collapsing, ribs closing around his heart. You knew he was meat then—just dead, dead, dead.

We Texans were dumbstruck. We didn't move. We watched the scooter tumble against a building, its throttle still whining. Then we watched Roy Rogers roll down the street and pop up in fright, his eyes wild and thyroid.

"Shit," LBJ said. There were tears on his cheeks, but he wasn't bawling. "Shit."

. . .

Soc Trang was Ozville when we got back. Blood rushed up to me first thing. I was as unfeeling as ice and stared deep into his blue eyes the whole minute he yattered. Tong was doing his thing again, Blood explained. The Captain had my blouse knotted up in his shaking fists. I'd gotten a gook, all right, but not Tong. His brother maybe, a cousin perhaps—but not Himself.

That was all LBJ needed.

"I ain't Texan no more," he said, jumping away from me. You could tell he was upset over Poetry's unhappy end. Then LBJ did some jive Hawaiian hip rolls and skedaddled. Next day he was King Ataful, High Mucky-Muck of Honolulu—as far from Texas and Poetry and death as he could get. You'd see him at the crapper or following mess, bare-chested, his brow darkening and growing like a shelf over his eyes. By week's end he had an unlived-in face.

"It ain't you, John Wayne," he said one day. "You look me up next year. I'll be the one on the beach with all the wahinis and surfboards. I got a big interest in self-preservation."

I was touched.

Several nights later more sad news:

"Bye-bye, John Wayne." That was Cisco and Pancho, rotating out to the World, their hitches expired. It was a moment of high melodrama: the three of us hemming and sadly scratching our boots in the dirt. They gave me heavy Mexican bear hugs. It was the famous scene among combat buddies of leave-taking, sentimental and brave. "Well, *adiós,*" they said, voices cracking, and I watched from the hooch as they trudged toward the tarmac airstrip, knowing I was alone and empty of loved ones and pals.

•   •   •

In no time I was as carefree and indifferent as a rock. Right after the departure of my friends, I got a bullhorn from Blood so Tong and I could have nightly debates. Blood thought I was marvelous and mad, the perfect grunt. I didn't care. Unwashed and unshaved and profoundly angry, I'd bound out to the perimeter around midnight, a giggly and expectant Blood at my elbow. We'd stand there in the dark, Blood already fingering his promotion. "Horn," I'd say. "Right-o, Tump." And Blood would slap that horn in my hand and stand aside.

After a deep breath, I'd tie into Tong, fifteen, twenty minutes at a time. Sometimes my remarks were prepared, sometimes not. I ridiculed him mightily, concentrating on his courage and sexual proficiency. Blood was thrilled. "Hot damn, Tump! Get him again, boy. You a marvel and a joy forever!" He had a Cong–American dictionary and kept feeding me choice phrases about destiny, idealism, and the celebrated rice diet. "Try this one, Tump: *Thang-mao phu cooch.*" It meant "Your momma farts in a balloon."

Poetry, I'm sure, would have been delighted. There I was, night after night, lungs busting, bellowing in the rain and the wind and the *rain.* I called Tong everything: queer, piss-ant, sore loser and other names I'd learned from Sandman. Blood even threw in some Arkansas witticisms.

Tong was almost speechless, content mainly to slander my daddy and my momma and my unborn white babies. First night he picked on the interstate highway system and one man, one vote. But you could tell his heart wasn't in it.

Then I started out after him.

That first night I was high on "33" beer and thoughts of revenge. Before I left, Blood held me up as an example to all. "Hip-hooray!" he shouted, being corny. All the troopers looked at him, then went loco too.

All night I walked in the bush, slapping flies and chasing shadows. I was a clown, I'm sure, barking and singing and whistling. The jungle was a lively place that night, with hooting and bug-noise from every corner, but the knowledge that I was out humping through the nest of the enemy was enough to lift my heart. At last I came upon that spot where I'd zapped those two Cong. Everything had changed. It was as if I'd stepped onto another planet. There was no evidence of damage, no bullet-scarred trees, etc. The ground was undisturbed and sweet-smelling. Oh, no, I thought. It wasn't awe or wonder that went through me at that moment; it was fear. I could feel the little links of my spine growing chill, freezing one by one until a whole age of ice crept up my back and closed around my throat like a collar. It was then I felt the bottom go out of me and knew I didn't want to kill Tong. I just wanted to see him—as if he were Westmoreland or the governor of Texas or the Abominable Snowman.

I got my chance the next night.

· · · ·

Like I told Li Dap, the NVA colonel I surrendered to on Highway 14 after it was over, that night was comedy. I went out about 0100 hours, Captain Blood having given me a slap of good wishes on the back.

"Take care, Tump," he said. Maybe he knew I wasn't coming back, I don't know.

"Yes, sir."

And then I was gone, slipping out as if passing through a seam in the universe. First thing I did, not ten clicks into the woods, was set aside my Sixteen, leaning it softly against a tree and retreating from it in chagrin. Next went my fatigues and flak jacket, right down to my skivvies and boots. (Li Dap said my near nudity is what saved me from being hacked to shreds by his regulars; he said that they thought I was some gringo coconut monk or an End-of-the-World Vision, too lame and feebleminded to eliminate.)

But that evening I felt grand. I was almost in Texas again, it felt, stomping through the Brownfield City Park, without worry and at peace. For an hour I walked or smoked or sat listening. I could hear everything—bugs breathing and mating, blossoms snapping open with a crack, and banyan trees rotting in noisy splendor. Poetry was right: life was easy. And it was good, too, full of many degrees of joy, etc.

As usual, Tong came on without warning.

"Good morning, pigs and baby killers of America."

Tong was vintage Enemy that night, deeply principled. He said it had been a superior week for the Good Guys, meaning him and his. They'd done damage, inflicted hardship. I was moving by this time, crawling and creeping in the military fashion. Of course, his voice seemed everywhere, sound dribbling down in that three-canopy jungle like a spring shower. To be true, I was jumpy and pleasantly scared, as if I were ten and playing Cowboys and Indians. It was like I was hunting my friends Jay Bullard and Joe Ben Newell up by the ditch bank or cane field.

Then I spotted him. Spotted his feet, actually, dangling

from a perch high overhead. I gave a start, feeling my heart slam into my neck.

For a time I just circled below, seeing his tiny feet twitch and cross, all the while his voice echoing musically. I tried to imagine his face, but all I came up with were the old familiars: Blood and Poetry, even Filth.

At last I stopped, breathing hard and truly exhilarated.

"Mr. Charles," I whispered, raising my empty hands in a rifle pantomine.

"Ah," Tong was saying, "bad news for Tump Walker."

But I wasn't listening, just squeezing my ears shut and feeling my chest swell with the fresh air of my future. He could've been talking about someone else.

DRIVING
HIS
BUICK
HOME

It was the summer I quit Coca-Cola in Brownfield, Texas, and my stepfather, Duke (full name: Earl Pinder), took up golf at the Mimbres Valley Country Club in Deming. He invited me over, said he'd rent me a full set of Wilson Pro-Staff irons, buy me a links-worthy pair of Foot-Joys.

"I see you in brown and white spikes," he said, "with that little flap over the laces. We'll be the Dynamic Duo—Batman and Robin. Make a ruckus in this hole, what do you say?"

He had a note in his voice I didn't recognize but which, if heard on a street hereabouts, might make you think twice. What's more, he had a day of Cutty Sark in him.

"C'mon," he said, "it'll take you—what?—six, maybe seven hours."

I couldn't, I told him. I had an interview in Olney. Texaco was looking for wise guys who could tote crates and be cheerful taking orders.

"Chuck," he said, "for an adult, you're mighty dense, aren't you?"

The next day he was sober. "I feel great," he said. "Listen to this." You could hear yips and grunts, heavy thuds and whacks—all of it echoing in his TravelBilt thirty-six-foot trailer. It was the first thing he bought when he started selling Chevrolets for Buzz King on Iron Street and began courting my mother. "This is Korean hand-to-hand," he was saying. "Sleepy's been teaching me. He's part dink—Filipino, maybe—he says I got a month of hard work ahead, then he gives me a belt and a robe and I'm ready." Duke said he'd thrown off a number of burdens lately, including the temptation to flop infantlike on the floor and be lunatic. Plus, he'd shot his dog, a frantic pound-breed named Chester.

"That animal had become a carouser, Chuck. I couldn't take it. He'd come in looking drag-ass, truly whipped. It brought out the anger in me."

"Put my mother on," I said.

There was a pause, into which rushed what my sweetheart, Trudy Weaver, calls Certain Knowledge. "Certain Knowledge," she claims, "is never good." It is knowledge, as I understand it, that has to do with pain and the wrecks we humans are because of it.

"No can do," Duke said. "Ivy's gone." She'd left a week ago last Wednesday, took the Toyota. He'd been next door at Sleepy and Carla's, playing gin rummy, watching the Miss Universe pageant on cable. "Lordy, Chuck, she took everything, even a double broiler."

I think now I had expected this, more or less. Among her neighbors when I was growing up—ladies named Winona and Darlene and Audrey Jo—my mother, Ivy Tinney Walker Pinder, was famous for doing exactly what she wanted. When

I was eight, she went off to California to see the NHRA Winternationals because she'd seen drag racer Shirley Muldowney on TV and liked that woman's brave, pink-outfitted approach to speed. When I was eleven, she put over four thousand dollars into a ballet school and divorced my real father the same day. "I'm a go-getter," she used to tell her lady friends. "I don't take grief from no man."

"Listen to this," Earl was saying. He read a note from my mother, two pages (he said), about the damndest things: waste, human dirts, failures. It was a catalogue of complaints, from kitchen and toilet behavior to what she called Higher Themes—namely, wants and private urges.

"She's forty-six years old," Duke was saying. "What's she going to do in Las Vegas, Nevada?"

"I can be there tomorrow," I said.

"What about Texaco?"

Didn't get it, I told him. I'm the squat sort, with the impressive shoulders and smart-alecky attitude of the left outside linebacker I was in college.

"What do you like, Chuck?" The edge was out of his voice now. "I'm an expert at chicken à la king. Maybe we'll eat Mex. How you feel about tacos?"

That night, after the ten-o'clock news out of Lubbock, I told Trudy that I'd be taking the bus over to Deming, stay a week, possibly two. Duke was depressed, and wasn't cheerful company what relatives were for?

"You know how I feel about him," she said.

I liked him, I said. Often more than I liked my mother. He had generosity in him. He was like Chester, his dog—neglectful and mostly heedless.

"You go," she said, "maybe I won't be here when you get back."

She was standing in the doorway to the bathroom, and I could see the smart LPN outfit she expected to wear tomorrow. She had a farm girl's meaty body and a sharp mind that would astound the shitkickers I'd grown up with. Plus, she seemed inclined to put up with me until I found out what in this life I was meant to do.

"Duke's got what he deserves," she said. "You stay out of it."

I'd be back in a week, I told her.

"You just have to do this, don't you?" She looked at me curiously, as if she'd discovered a character trait I didn't deserve to have, and my heart did something sudden and heavy.

"I'll be at Debbi's," she said. "She's got a brother, you know."

. . .

When I arrived, Duke was behind the trailer, tinkering with his car. It was several tons of chrome, a Buick one family could live from.

"What do you think?" he asked. "Sleepy calls it my poonmobile. I get me some spade whitewalls and I'm fixed."

I was impressed, its finish a shine that comes only with elbow grease and real love.

"Check the upholstery," he said. "It's Carla's idea. That's kangaroo leather, Chuck. Number one, imported, very expensive."

I held up my duffel bag and windbreaker. "Where do I put my stuff?"

"Bedroom," he said. "I like the couch. Been watching mucho TV."

Duke looked like too many of the men Ivy had dated when

I was in junior high—the loose skin sloth creates, worry lines around the eyes, an embarrassing shoulder sag.

"Look at this." Over his greasy overalls, he'd thrown on a knee-length fur coat. "Rabbit," he said, grinning. "When it turns cold, I'll be one slick character, right?"

The inside of his trailer brought out the neatness need I suffer from, and I was predisposed to bring a hose or torch in there. On the kitchen counter were stacks of Folger's cans stuffed with coupons. A rack of racy Florida shirts hung in the bathroom door. His melmac dishes were in the tub, and you could tell his meals were mainly fat-heavy inventions served in red sauce. It was grim. Books were scattered all over. "Fine, inspirational stuff," he told me later. "You read this, you get a permanent uplift." One was called *Mother's Reference Book of Glorious Verse.* It mentioned "experience," then provided a dozen definitions for "luck." Ivy's handwriting had defaced it thoroughly. On the bedroom walls were photos of houses he'd been the labor for, including dozens in Laos and Cambodia years ago, when he worked for a Des Plaines contractor employed by the USIA and Air America.

Outside, still in his coat, Duke was talking to a short, skinny guy in khaki trousers and a Taiwan jacket that said "Death from Above."

"Hey, Chuck. Meet Sleepy."

His real name was Irwin Floyd, and he was as white as a Safeway frozen chicken.

"Say something in French," Duke told him. "Sleepy's profound," I heard. "He's a certified genius."

Sleepy's voice had a whine you might mistake for music— mostly nose with his meager chest thrown in for emphasis.

"What'd he say?" I wondered.

It was, Duke claimed, how-do-you-do, kiss-my-ass, taxi-to-the-market, how-much-darling. "The usual stuff," Duke said, smiling. "Sleepy picked it up in Saigon. Do some more, Sleepy."

The man was fine at imitations too. That afternoon, he showed us a pigeon, a stallion Flicka might like and selected human beings—Georgie Jessel, Dizzy Dean, Ed Sullivan. "He's working on an act," Duke told me. We were sitting in the shade of Sleepy's trailer, our backs against the cinder-block skirting. In the distance, the desert shimmered, heat waves rising, and it was possible to believe that all of New Mexico, even the parts tourists love, was a geographic nightmare of rock and weed I was glad I didn't live in anymore.

"Do Daffy Duck," Duke was saying. Then to me: "This man's an inspiration to me, Chuck. Been keeping me going."

Around five, a Biscayne lurched between the trailers and stopped, a cloud of dust boiling up.

"That's Carla," Duke said.

Instantly, Sleepy was up, mouth in overdrive, moving as if he'd been bitten or truly frightened.

"What's he saying?" I asked.

Duke didn't know. "Love talk, maybe. This is a very romantic couple, Chuck."

Now and then I'd catch a word, something sensible and not especially spit filled.

"Sleepy's got some Marine vet crap," Duke said. "He's a beautiful person inside. So's Carla."

Carla was all lips and hair. She'd have been at home anywhere, the North Pole, Never-never land, ten thousand miles from this place. To be true, I could see some Ivy in her, particularly around the eyes, which had enough dark in them to be called sly. Both women also had an affection for powerful makeup and the perfume to match it. She was wearing a sea-green beautician's outfit, thin enough to see her underwear through.

"You're Ivy's kid, right?"

"I mentioned you were coming," Duke said.

Sleepy hung at Carla's side like a stone, and I figured he was from a part of the world I'd never see.

"What kind of nose is that?" she said.

Intellectual, I told her, from my biological dad, Theodore Walker. I had other talents—from Ivy's genes—the high forehead, Jughead's ears. Once upon a time I could run very fast, and I was still pretty loyal.

"Let's eat," Duke put in. "I'm starved."

We ended up at the Thunderbird Lounge next to the bowling alley. Duke was in fine spirits, the company just the ticket to keep his smile lit. "Make a muscle, Carla," he said once. "Carla lifts weights. She's a jewel." At ten, Uncle Roy and his Red Creek Wranglers appeared on the small stage. Roy, Duke said, was a special pal of his. (It was an obvious untruth: Roy had that unwholesome glint in his eyes which said he was a friend to no one.)

"Play 'Love and the Hurt of It,'" Duke called out. He was in the mood, he said, for some real foot-stomping. "I'm in my element," he announced. "Ivy never liked to come here; she preferred the Ramada Inn."

Duke danced with Carla, looking inappropriately light on his feet for a guy over fifty. I did my wolf howl, the thing I learned as rowdy TeKE; I made a dozen frat-derived noises. "Shake that money-maker," Sleepy yelled. When he hollered it in French, it didn't sound nearly as encouraging. Around midnight Duke went to the center of the dance floor and did some karatelike moves Elvis probably invented; you could see he was satisfying his life-affirming instincts.

"Roy," he said, his shirt with the pineapples on it now sweat-soaked and droopy, "do you know anything with glee in it?"

It was then Carla tapped me on the shoulder.

"That was a low thing Ivy did," she said.

. . .

The rest of our week was what Carla called a frenzy of sport and drink. Before noon, Sleepy, Duke and I went to the golf course, nine holes of sun-scorched bent Bermuda and thousands of acres of gnarly mesquite trees, a layout we are likely to find on Mars once we land there. The first morning Duke told the pro, J. Benson Newell, to put me in the finest duds.

"I want him to look like Gene Sarazen," he said.

Sleepy was strictly in modern dress, an outfit that brought up the words "Cuban" and "felon." Duke, by contrast, looked like a happy champion from the pages of *Golf Digest*—all in peach and magenta and chartreuse, the effect of it extremely cruel on the eyes.

"In the next life," Duke said, "I'm coming back as a gigolo. Get to dress swanky and be friendly with the upper crust."

We drank that week—Calvert and Oso Negro that Duke had driven up from Palomas. "Ivy liked panty-waist drinks," he said one morning. "She believed in syrups, I think. Jesus." He, however, believed in a higher form of intoxicant. Liquor, he told us on the first tee, had many purposes, foremost of which was solace. He was yelling to be heard above the wind and showing us the spot, a lightning-zapped cottonwood at the dogleg, he hoped his ball would reach.

"Don't nobody interrupt me now," he said. "I'm gonna smash the living shit out of this here Maxfli."

On the next tee, Sleepy announced that he himself was a true-blue cynic.

"Me too," Duke said.

I was thinking about Trudy: what breakfast looks like in front of her, her Texas nightwear, the day sounds she makes getting up. I remembered how she kissed—like a Taurus, which is paper-dry and in a hurry to move on.

"The hard core, that's what I believe in," Sleepy said. "You learn that in Two Corps, the straightshooting and all." He appeared to have put himself together in the dark, and from a box. "I'm an educated *hombre,* too. I went to UTEP, an ag major," he said. "Man, I didn't learn diddly there."

"That's right," Duke said.

Sleepy believed in getting and having and keeping and knowing one's own strengths.

"I could listen to this for hours," Duke told me.

On the green, Sleepy listed his beliefs. "One," he said, "don't ever be the last to leave. Two, take love where you can. Three, don't let a friend fool you twice. Four, nobody's on nobody's side. A-men."

"Christ," Duke said. I believed he was near tears. "I do miss that woman, I really do."

That afternoon, while Duke worked on his Buick, I called home. I finally found Trudy at Tricia's, one of her Texas Tech pals and no fan of mine. "Don't worry," she said, "I haven't done anything with Bucky. He's gross. Besides, he's a liar." I could hear party noises in the background, very strange rock 'n' roll that put me in mind of why I prefer what cowboys compose. There was probably weed going around too.

"You got a letter," she said. "That place in Goree said you should drive over for an interview."

"That's the Holly plant," I told her. "We'd have to move."

You could hear a male hollering, then a loud whump-whump that could have been a chair tipping over.

"Your mother called," Trudy said. "She told you not to worry. She was a little disappointed you were with Duke."

"What's she doing?"

According to Trudy, Ivy now resided in the lap of plush. She'd already found a companion, a faro dealer named Hover. "He's in the Vegas book, if you want to call. She doesn't regret anything, of course, not even sneaking off."

"What's that noise?" I asked.

"That's Cleve Pounds. He wants my sandals, it's a party game."

I told her I'd be home that weekend. Earlier if possible.

"Don't come Friday," she said. "We're going swimming at the Bottomless Lakes."

Before I hung up, I heard another voice—this what plants probably have in their own world—asking for silence.

Through the window I could see Duke and Sleepy sitting in the front seat of the Buick, the doors open. They had a body language I believe in, and it said that from the direction they were watching, south toward Mexico, would come the riches they wished for most.

"When I pop off in her," Sleepy was saying, "it's clean. I get dizzy."

"High mountains," Duke said. "With me and Ivy, it was altitude."

At the Thunderbird that night Carla wanted to dance with me. "What's that?" she said. It was a step Trudy had taught me, and I was proud of the accomplishments of my rear end. "Looks terrible," she said. Sleepy and Duke sat at their usual table, glassy-eyed and slumped. Once, Sleepy did an imitation of me: it involved unsubtle thighwork but good intentions toward the feet. "I thought I was better than that," I said. "No, sir," Duke told me, "that's your charm." He was wearing his rabbit coat again and I had to believe he was being good-natured.

On the slow dance, Carla held me close. "You think I'm pretty?" she wondered. I did. "It's my smile. I keep my eyes open wide. Most people don't. They're the ones with wrinkles."

On the stage, Uncle Roy looked to be suffering, and I entertained the idea that, without much fuss, I could get Duke out of there and home. Given a relaxed attitude and my heavy driving foot, we could be in Las Vegas by the next evening.

"Your girl got hair like mine?" Carla was asking.

I'd met Trudy a year ago, I told her, at the Mile 49 bar outside Tatum. We had much in common—our ages, certain sci-fi authors, how loving ought to be—but few opinions about what appeared on heads nowadays.

"My best feature ain't my hair," Carla announced. "It's just part of the package, the arrangement."

At their table, Sleepy was speaking French again, his chitchat pulpy and expressed with considerable spit. I caught a few words: "Vietnam," "gunship," "Barry Goldwater."

"We're thinking about moving," Carla was saying. "I've got some opportunities elsewhere."

That night, before we turned in, Duke came into the bedroom.

"Tell me how I look." He was wearing Jockey shorts and had a fallen belly I would be pleased not to inherit. "I got the suspicion I look real bad."

"You're in great shape," I told him. "Honest."

"A year from now, you won't know me." He stood especially erect, one part of him watching the others. "Think of me with a moustache like Burt Reynolds. Let my hair grow a touch too. My body, I can't do nothing about."

The next day—and for three days after—Duke was sick. "It's my bronchial tree," he wheezed. "I had asthma as a kid. Breathing can be a bitch sometimes." He lay on the couch in his underwear, watching TV and drinking V8 juice. "I used to have a philosophy once," he said. I was eating Corn Chex at the coffee table. The wind had been up since daybreak, dust spraying against the trailer like buckshot. "I used to believe in the impossible. Then I went to work for the post office." He looked at me, hard. "That's a joke, Chuck."

Duke was Ivy's second husband. He'd shown up when I was a junior in high school but didn't want to be my pal. He sent me off to TCU for three miserable semesters (too much pocket billiards and TeKE high jinks) and didn't complain when I bailed out to take up residence in Brownfield. He gave me five hundred dollars one time after I got fired for spitting on a bald Hillside Dairy night supervisor whose respect I had not earned. Another time, the day after my real dad died, Duke drove over, got me drunk, and let me be bitter-acting for a time.

In the afternoon, we watched *The Price Is Right*, in which the MC gave away goodies I hope to bring home to Trudy Weaver one day: a stereo, a honeymooners' trip to Hawaii, what America's contemporary living rooms have. Then we spent an hour studying a soap opera in which everybody, youngster through adult, was either diseased, crazy, pent up or afflicted by the compulsion to think out loud.

"I love it," Duke said. "Some days I just sit and roar. You ask Sleepy."

Toward evening, he'd worked his way through a stack of magazines, each yellow and well-fingered. "Listen to this," he hollered once. *"Her bodice reeked with flower smut, the overpowering odors of magnolia and mint. Yancey could stand it no longer. His brain reeling, he leapt for her throat, his tongue an instrument of pain and joy."*

I hadn't heard stuff like that since going as a kid to the beauty shop with Ivy, long before she met Duke.

He read me several, each full of flight and movement in exotic locales, all seized by sentiment the immature mind is said to cleave to. "Here's another," he said, reading a paragraph in which the heroine—a Lake Charles, Louisiana, aristocrat named Pearl—was swept up, done dirty by the inventive use of legcraft, repaired by the whisper of the right words, and then dragged out to be lesson-taught.

"Exceptional," Earl yelled, phlegm coming up.

My favorite was "The Inventory of Love" by D. F. "Doc" Sweeny, which Duke called the best damned hour's entertainment he'd had in weeks. Doc could do it all, he said: swarming and being overcome, a thrill that snatched the breath away. In addition, it had scheming, back-stabbing, and enough pointy-headed vocabulary to make it serious.

"Read me that bosom part again," Duke said. His face wore the shine of everything but vigor.

At ten-thirty, Sleepy knocked at our door.

"What do you think of this?" he asked. He rolled his shoulders, slumped himself in a fashion I hadn't seen since Wildcat football practice years ago.

"What's it supposed to be?" I asked.

He had his cheeks puffed out, eyebrows lowered. "Nixon."

"I think it sucks," Duke told him.

"Me too," Sleepy said. "Needs work."

.   .   .

Somewhere in here I called Ivy long-distance. The Vegas directory had four Hovers. The first didn't answer. The second owned an answering machine with a voice too breathy for what I thought Ivy liked. Number three picked up right away.

"Florence, I know this is you." His was an agitated voice, and immediately I came up with the picture of a guy who irons his pajamas. "Don't do this anymore, Florence," he was saying. "I've told the phone company about you. There is a law against annoyance, you know."

I had the urge, felt in the throat, to throw aside the phone and trust it would hang itself up.

"Is Ivy there?"

He was having Certain Knowledge now, and it was making him feel like a fool.

"Who is this?"

I could be cute, or I could not. "Uncle Roy."

"Hey," he said. "Well, hey there."

I could tell he wanted to go on, give me his life story.

"Listen," I said, "tell her I called, okay?"

"Any message?"

I looked around the trailer. Duke was out back, hitting a bucket of practice balls Sleepy had stolen from the driving range, and I was trying to tidy up. Right then, the Eureka vacuum looked terribly important to me, and I conceived of myself in an hour standing in a room I'd made shine myself.

"No," I told him, "no message."

.   .   .

On Friday, Duke spent the afternoon in his car. He'd crank it up, rev the motor a few times, switch it off. He was reading another D. F. Sweeny story, "What Can Change Anything on Earth." I'd read it the night before, didn't approve. It was long on moralisms and too slow to compete with the angry Arabs

Ted Koppel had on. Plus, it used words Duke's dictionary didn't have, and this phrase: "a dither of regret."

When it got quiet out there, I peeked out the window. Sleepy was standing next to the car, looking hangdog and sullen. His face had no one in it but himself—not George Burns or Howard Cosell or Johnny Mathis. All I could hear was the pair of them swearing. "Shit," Sleepy would say. A beat later, you heard Duke: "Crap." Sleepy was in his Air Cav costume again, his hair in the afternoon glare giving off an almost green glow. He wasn't a dink at all; he was from Pluto.

"Goddamn," he was saying.

An instant later, Duke was out of the car, hugging the little guy. Sleepy was lost in Duke's arms; he didn't know what to do, hug back or cringe. "Squeeze," I was saying to myself. "Grab on, you piss-ant." He ended up patting Duke's bare back—daintily, as if he were petting a strange animal, one with inflamed eyeballs and sharp wet teeth.

"Holy moly," Duke said. "Jumping Jesus."

When Sleepy went back to his trailer, Duke sat again in the car, tapping the steering wheel. I couldn't see his face, but that fingering told you all you needed to know about several unhappy emotions we can have. I was going to holler out, when Carla appeared, in her beautician's uniform, her hair a high complex tangle a man like D. F. "Doc" Sweeny would find meaningful.

"Well," I said to myself, my hand shaking in the dishwater. "Well, well, well."

Carla was all over him in a flash, hugging and squeezing and kissing his cheek. Draped around him, she looked at home.

"For crying out loud," Duke said.

"Right on," Carla said. "Sorry."

I counted to one hundred before he came inside and flopped

down on the sofa, mouth-breathing. I was standing next to a shelf of his knickknacks I'd organized, big to little. I figured this was the way he looked when Ivy left, his face muscles slack, his crumpled internal self visible even to the dumbest or most carefree.

"You think there's anything like fortune?" he asked. "I think there's people with it, which is fine, and those without, which is sorry."

You could tell it was merely talk. French talk.

"I ain't a cynic," he said.

"I knew you weren't," I told him. "You're like me, an optimist. We always look on the bright side." Christ, I didn't know what I was saying.

"They're moving," he told me. "Carla has a job waiting for her in El Paso. She's going to be boss, the White House department store. It's an opportunity." Sleepy was the tag-along kind, he said. He'd go anywhere. He made pals easily, had the gift. Must've been a hundred U.S. gyrenes through their trailer the last few years.

"You got the gift too," I said.

He was looking at the place on one curtain rod where his rabbit coat had hung until yesterday (I'd put it in his closet), and it occurred to me to speak up now. Something small and fragile, possibly bonelike, had given loose inside me.

"I feel lousy," he said. "Everything was so nice."

He could live with us, I said. We had an extra room. He could move out Trudy's pottery, live the life of Riley. He'd have his own bathroom, could come and go as he wished.

"Nah," he said. "I got a funny feeling about that girl."

"We got a great golf course there. Cheap green fees, Julius Boros supposedly played on it."

The focus had left his eyes: they had all the appeal of two marbles in the bottom of a water glass. "What're they gonna do down there? Carla, I can understand. She's always talking about being thwarted, about getting the short end. She's good at what she does."

My mind sought a thousand things at once, none having to do with his neighbors or how they might fare in life.

"Sleepy's gonna open a school, teach karate, kung-fu. He thinks maybe there's a market for that."

"You cold?" I said.

His shoulders were twitching.

"Maybe I'll get a tattoo," he said. "I had a friend once, back in Enid. Had the Preamble to the Constitution on his back, no kidding. Said it was a source of strength and something else." Duke rubbed his chin. "Courage, I think. He was a dumb sucker, though. He died."

"Let's go to the Thunderbird." I had put down my dishrag. "I'm hungry."

It was then, while he was hauling himself off the couch, his face plain with what I think of as innocence, that he said, "I didn't shoot Chester." Duke regarded his hands as if they held a surprise for him. "I just said that. He ran off. Didn't like the cuisine, I guess." Duke was putting on another dramatic shirt, this one an aggressive display of island fruit and those weird birds that eat it. "That dog comes back, though, I don't care where he's been, I'm gonna be very angry. Gonna blow his ass away for sure."

.   .   .

In the morning, he told me to take his Buick back. "I got my eye on a Datsun pickup," he said. "It came in the other day for a new Caprice."

"You sure?"

He grabbed my hand, shook it happily.

"I'm glad you came," he said.

Sleepy and Carla's trailer already looked deserted, but I had the impression that, given the way our world works, I'd be seeing them again one day.

"Tell Ivy, if you see her, no hard feelings."

In five minutes I was out of town, driving 70-80 instead of the interstate. Duke's Buick was a marvel, its interior of gizmos a delight to the tinker's mind I have. I'd be home in seven hours, give or take. Trudy and I would go to the Pizza Hut, then she'd ask what happened. I'd mention this and that, touch upon the high moments, set the scene a bit. We'd be as we were the day after we'd met—tender-minded and ignorant of Certain Knowledge. Then I'd kiss her, and we'd go on from there.

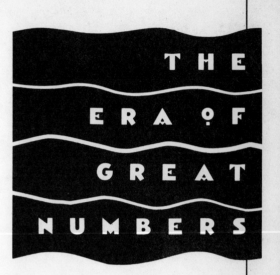

THE
ERA OF
GREAT
NUMBERS

Head coach Woody Knapp stood in the center of his office, a manorial layout that put him in mantic frame of mind. He had parquet floors, coromandel screens, a cream brocade sectional sofa, a mile of Marie Antoinette moldings. Through a window which opened onto the players' locker room, he saw backfield coach Nate Creer methodically beating a sophomore second-string scatback named Krebs. Coach Knapp had one thought, possibly warmhearted, about the relationship of discipline to pedagogy; and another, this about what it meant to play football in the twenty-first century.

Near his desk his publicist, Lefty Mantillo, was on the phone, answering questions from a reporter for a special issue of *Jane's Fighting Ships*.

"They wonder if you'll use the Umayyad," Lefty said, "and how gravitons might complement the game plan."

Coach Knapp watched Nate Creer pummeling the benchwarmer. Groans were heard, as were thumps and bone-noise. He was reminded of the Turner painting of Piazza San Marco, *Juliet and Her Nurse.*

"Tell them I agree with Einstein," Coach Knapp said. "Football, like nature, is simple and beautiful."

Lefty had come to the team from the night world of rock 'n' roll. He had made famous The Unfinished Business of Childhood, a band that took turmoil as a theme to speak for the beleaguered.

"They're interested in the pregame meal," Lefty said.

Coach adjusted his tie. It was silk, crafted by the adjunct faculty in the Division of Careless Movements.

"Mango sorbet," Coach began. "A milk concoction."

"They like that," Lefty told him.

Coach read the rest: West Beach Café taquito, beignets, grillades, Mardi Gras King cake, hearts-of-palm salad, Cat Château Petrus, lobster medallions and rosettes of chestnut puree.

"One more question," Lefty said.

Lefty had the bald, thickly veined egghead of a B-movie Martian. He was said to have had in the old days an affiliation with the Montonero guerrillas of Argentina, a single-minded group with an explicit interest in hemispheric chaos.

"They want to know the pregame talk," Lefty was saying. "Chapter and verse, your perspective."

The pregame talk, Coach announced, would be the usual—about grief, how it is total and deep. "As I see it," he concluded, "we have three choices: move, ascend or vanish."

Nate Creer was finished with his player. Coach Knapp saw a puddle on the floor—necessary private fluids, perhaps—and he heard the sound of something pulpy, but in cleats, scraping toward the showers.

"Remember," Coach said, "truth is indifferent and men with guns are everywhere."

When Creer entered the room, Lefty exited in a flourish. Creer had been with Coach Knapp from the beginning, the intramural squads in the Louisiana playing fields of the Organization of American States. His virtues were a scientist's attention to detail, plus the wry imagination of a sneak-thief. He was thought to have a wife somewhere—in the First Republic of Albuquerque?—whose face had the texture of igneous rock.

"What was that beating all about?" Coach asked.

"Sloth," Creer said. "I spoke about digging deep within the self. I used the words 'ontology' and 'entelechy.' I appealed to the old conventions of manhood, of self-worth. I respected our differences within the mutuality of shared purpose. I aimed to address the issues of sacrifice, which leads to the loftimost, and puerilism, which does not. Then I pounded the stuffings out of him."

Coach Knapp picked up his briefcase, his silver whistle. "You mentioned Aquinas, I trust. And Vasco da Gama."

Nate Greer nodded. "Lordy," he said, "I love it when they smartmouth."

Woody Knapp walked through the locker room slowly. The air was stale, yellow, heavy. Several odors reached him: unguents, ointments, salves. His people, his players, were monodonists, ligubriates, inspired by Saracens. They spoke Igorot, Kimbundu, fluent New Orleans. Missing eyes, ears, toes, one or two limbs, they believed in firmaments, unified fields, what infants yearn for. In one locker, he noticed a two-page discussion of spasm-dose ratios, nuclear throw-weights; in another, a beaded reticule. He could see skull caps, djellabas, a garter belt, a life-size china snow leopard. They wore shawls, prophylacteries, vinyl jumpsuits. Coach Knapp heard a tape player somewhere, a tune called "More Facts About Life." It mentioned the pineal gland, what to do with the floccose. Like snowfall in July, its effect was eerie. One wall—this of Pentelic marble—was covered with graffiti unique to the intimate acts of man: birth, death, sport. The gods here were Cytrons and Maronites, metal constructions from the firms of Mattel and Fisher-Price in the old ages; and the atmosphere seemed basinesque, Caribbean, having to do with body-whomping and sly ways of using sweat. It brought to mind flickering torches, low but constant fevers, what can be accomplished by heedlessness.

At the entrance to the tunnel that led under the stands to the stadium, Coach Knapp met Eppley Franks, the editor of the alumni quarterly, *The Vulgate*. He was the ghostwriter for Coach's autobiography, *The Era of Great Numbers*.

"I got the galleys back yesterday," Franks was saying. His eyes were full of flecks and various luminous colors. In addition to talk linking him to specific jungle-spawned narcotics, he was said to like all things thalloid and most spore-bearing creatures.

"They want to delete the chain mail," he was saying. "They're in conference now about the anga coats and Mrs. K's silk turban. Textiles upset them."

"What do they want to substitute?"

Eppley Franks pawed through a folder of documents at his feet. His was the handwriting of an Ostrogoth, but he had the virtue of a prose style direct enough to cause excruciating pain.

"There's talk of Huns, Hittites. I heard the name Ramses Two once. There's concern with subtext. 'Despotic' is a word that gets mentioned a lot."

"Where do we stand on this?" Coach wondered.

Eppley Franks glanced at his notes. At one time he'd apparently written on ox hide.

"Statute supports us on this one. We have Bishop De Quadra, Lord Robert. Prothalamion's our big gun. They, of course, control the paper and ink."

Coach Knapp was watching the cheerleaders practicing in the near end-zone. They seemed to have come from the only cities in the world: Islamabad and Trenton, New Jersey. Lithe and sufficiently buxom, they had a cheer artful and acrobatic enough to serve increase and weal.

"Touch my hand," Coach said. "What do you hear?"

"I hear compromise," Franks said. "Expediency."

Coach was watching the smokes in the southern distances—pink and yellow and green. Fires were said to be still smoldering in El Paso. There were rumors of fierce, eccentric hot winds and the habits of displaced housewives. One heard stories—set in other regions of the baked, white deserts—of hungry dogs and the howling food fleeing them.

"One more thing, Coach."

The cheerleaders were chanting about gore.

"Speak to me, Eppley. I'm in a hurry."

"No more philosophizing, okay? I'm getting grief from just about everybody. Stick to the basics, they say. Carnage, things you've won, why everybody loves you."

. . .

In his observation tower near the fifty-yard line, Coach Knapp was approached by his defensive line coordinator, Teak Warden. His was the face of a monast—bony, hollow-eyed, mean. At his belt flopped a walkie-talkie.

"I am lonely," Teak said. In his manner was the suggestion of loud voices, hanging meat. "I like to toy with my food. I'm starting to hear songs. I'm beginning to assign gender to inanimate objects, concepts. A phrase keeps popping up: 'the curves of time.' I can't sleep, I fear my bedclothes."

On a scrimmage field beyond the open end of the stadium stood the marching band, practicing a brassy, optimistic composition, basic oom-pah-pah with a fair amount of human shrieking in it. They had instruments of hair, vinework, dried

fibers—flutes, bouzoukis, shells, bells. They liked to prance on
the field at halftime, all five hundred of them, to form words
or symbols. At the TCU game in Fort Worth, they'd spelled
out a single declarative sentence: *Being is not different from
nothingness.* They had names for man's slangy parts and knew
where angst came from.

"I'm working on a purer vision," Teak was saying. "I keep
seeing a place like this—vast, silent, full of rubble."

The walkie-talkie came to life: "Victor-Zulu-King, this is
Almighty, do you copy?"

In the distance, the clouds were beasts, serpents, civil ruin.

"I had a dream the other night," Teak said.

"Why are you telling me this?"

"It was profound. Religious. There was horror involved."

Down below, Coach's players were yammering in Pali,
Tamil, Oriya. Moving in slow motion, the linebackers raised
their fists, grunting. In helmets and pads, they brought to mind
vaulted cisterns, limestone caves, the lamps the holy worship
by.

"We're a serious people," Coach Knapp said.

Teak Warden nodded. "Ain't that the truth?"

"It's a lyric mode we seek, something to satisfy the animal
in us. Wistfulness extends, diminishes our purpose. There is
danger of ambiguity, of winding down."

The walkie-talkie crackled again: "Almighty, Almighty, this
is Victor-Zulu-King, we have contact. Repeat: we have contact,
do you copy?"

"These are sad times, Teak Warden," Coach said.

"The saddest."

A hot wind had come up, like jet exhaust.

"We're in a strange business."

"Affirmative," Teak Warden said.

"There is the laying on of hands," Coach said, "and the

hurling of bodies. Information is exchanged. We objectify, polarize. Screams are heard. There is hooting and other meaningful tumult."

"There are chains of being," Teak Warden said. "We are pre-science. I'm thinking matrix. I'm thinking the moral life, a negotiation of same."

Coach was watching the grandstands opposite him, tier upon tier of seats and gleaming metal benches. Plastered to the upper walls were banners from the pep club: "Refute Belief," "Visual Messages Are Not Discursive," "Self-Expression Requires No Artistic Form." There were impressive drawings from *Tractatus Logico-Philosophicus* and *The Ape and the Child.* Conference flags were whipping back and forth: Griffons, Knave-life, The Hidden Iman.

"Teak," Coach said, "who is that?"

He indicated a figure squatting beside a meager fire high up in the stands. It was a man, certainly, who seemed wrapped in a half-century of north-country outerwear.

The walkie-talkie hissed to life again. Someone was calling for help. "Accept no higher being," a voice said. "Let's go out there and thwart somebody."

"Don't know," Teak Warden said. "Student, possibly."

"Whose?"

Teak Warden waved, and yonder, out of the clothes, shot an arm. It snapped up and down several times, then disappeared. Something about it suggested delirium.

"Ours," Teak said, "definitely ours."

.   .   .

On the field, defensive line coach Archie Weeks, carrying a brushed-aluminum briefcase, had assembled his players in a semicircle. A dozen pens stuck out of his breast pocket. His

view of sport was admirably cerebral. He was now referring to
a chalkboard dense with numbers and letters, arrows and stars.
He was very nimble for someone who sweated and twitched.

"I want penetration," he was saying. "Give me an emotion,
lower organs. I want a rising up and a putting asunder."

His players—Cud, Onan, Redman, Univac, the Prince of
Darkness—were serious, attentive. They had majors from every
page in the catalogue: disquiet, vigor, happenstance. They were
beef with heads that swiveled a little.

"I take failure personally," Archie Weeks was saying. "I
want luridness out there tomorrow. Verve approaching mad-
ness."

Coach Knapp remained to one side. There would be several
more lectures by his assistants, then he would have to say
something. He was watching the mountains in the east. They
were called the Organs and seemed associated with conditions
best explained in poetry: rue, torment, befuddlement. Between
them and him—indeed, all around, from horizon to horizon—
lay the desert full of stunted trees, scrub, spines, thorns, savage
hooks. People were believed to be out there—tribes of very
unpleasant, dark-minded citizens. They had sores and mangy
pelts, and every now and then they roared out of the spectacu-
lar wastes to watch football.

"I'm talking about conspiracies," Archie Weeks was saying.
"Insinuations, betrayals. I'm talking about piling on, about
getting one's licks in."

Next was Gene Jenks, offensive line coach. He looked like
circus property. He had the need to lean into people's faces and
yowl.

Gene Jenks spoke of the ideal sportsman. A half-winged
creature, it could be any of the human colors, but it knew
everything: how wish works, what to say when the glands call.
It was a machine. Something with many fine parts. A quiet,

high-speed operation with uncommonly expressive shoulder-work. It had a chemical description and delightful physical properties. It had girth and heft, and slammed about in the current hubbub being heroic.

"Things could be worse," Gene Jenks said. "Things could be much worse."

Vigorous applause greeted Coach Knapp when he stepped to the center of his players. He had visited each of their homes—their tents, cabins, lean-tos, caves. He had seen what they'd eaten, how they'd prepared themselves, and they had confessed to him their joys, their nightmares. Mesomorphs, hairy, porcine, thick as tree stumps—they were all the ilks folks come in. They read Erasmus, Cato, referred to themselves as loin or chop. Many of them slept upright and appeared better for it. They had thick parts and amusing ways of getting from hither to yon. They did not mumble. Nor did they lose direction, wander off. One would address them and, at the signal, they would go. Footwear was vital to them, as were rigor and single-mindedness. What did one say to such beings? He had met their parents, their distant relations. He'd met their mates—names came to him: Lulu, Jo Ann, Dottie. These women were life principles and part of winning itself. Coach's players believed in ritual and magic. They carried lucky thread, well-thumbed coins, medals that promised protection against smite itself. They had special words: *miasma, columbine, Umgang.* They were held together—apart from the claim of the larger world—by tape and plastic, by miracle fabrics and bolts. One did not speak to them directly. One used an elaborate rhetoric of colors and numbers, a code of doing and being done to. "Blue, forty-six, slant left," one would say, and an instant later there would be a pile of very satisfied sportsmen. All over the fallen world such exchanges were being made: language became action and the human measure of it. Unusually large

men were speaking to almost round things and beating each
other for the sake of them. This was not war. It was earth and
wind, fire and water. It was biology and the shedding of un-
necessary parts. One said, "Red, dish-right, on eight," and
immediately there was a collision and the crawling away from
it.

"Sleep, eat, wash," Coach Knapp said, at last. "This is what
we do. When we work, life is easy. We get to go places and
hear ourselves talked about. This is what I like. Don't disappoint me."

. . .

In the locker room Coach Knapp came upon one of his people
reading a book. The player was a free safety—a former wood-
chopper named Herkie Walls, Coach believed—and he wore
a T-shirt with a picture of the new universe. There were curli-
cues, as well as runes, objects made important by desire. The
kind of collapsed, special ruin hope had once lived in.

"I have questions," the kid said. "I have doubts, grow depressed. My vocabulary's shrinking."

A wind had risen, steady and full of faraway dirts.

Coach Knapp gestured to the book: "What're you reading?"

Herkie Walls held the thing aloft, his playbook. It was open
to the pages relevant to humbug and derring-do.

"I could have been a thousand things," the kid said. His eyes
suggested fear. "For one birthday I received a field jacket. It
was khaki, its hem bordered with formal Kufic lettering. I
preferred to wear it with polychrome sateen. I had the need to
stand out and be incorrigible."

Tension was involved here, a wariness. Worry was one pa-
rameter of Coach's profession; faith, the other. Eleven, sometimes twelve times a year he ushered his people onto one turf

or another. He gave instructions, rules, rubrics. He urged them toward the manifest in themselves, put before them images of fleece and flax. He reminded his people what their opponents were: creatures without spawn, vermiculate matter that ambled on two legs. Coach Knapp created stories, narratives featuring a random collection of humans who find themselves in a remote, austere venue. In every version, the endings were identical: this collection—this cadre of gristle and girth—discovers unfamiliar and surprising things and returns to the world changed in some way.

"Where are you from, free safety?"

Almost black with blood, a hand appeared, pointed. "The Province of Florida, I think. You recruited me."

A light went on in Coach Knapp's memory. He saw—anew and in a way quite compelling—a thatched hut, a puny fire, a mewling thing. The common elements.

"I said you were a state of mind, I believe. I said if you ran very swiftly and were acceptably violent, you would be admired."

A smile came to the free safety, Herkie Walls. He had been bamboozled, the floor of his self given way, and now he was not.

"Thinking is a performing art, Coach. That's what you said."

Like father and son, they consulted the playbook. Its pages, light and precious as human skin, were garish with hexagons, exotic birds, palmette stars. Its language ran from border to border and defined the seat the self sits in. The product of a dozen minds, it avoided terms like "capitulation" and "surrender." Unlike the playbooks of the olden, icier ages—the times of Sooners and Razorbacks and Nittany Lions—this volume trafficked in parables, allegories, fables. It was to be read in a wild, silent place; it made the muscles tight and strong, set the

organs tingling. Among other things, it spoke of love, which
was the things that happened and what we said about them.
Though it mentioned sulphur and brimstone, what speeds the
stupid travel at, its effect was hortatory; its purpose, to heal and
to promote fellowship.

"So what do we know now?" Coach asked.

In the kid's open locker was fabric that recalled mirth and
what swine are for.

"We know one meaning of life," the kid said. "We've
learned to discriminate, not to be deflected or deferred."

"We have learned not to read between the lines," Coach
said. "To speak clearly and to hoist heavy things."

"Fucking A," the kid said.

. . .

Coach Knapp made his way across campus in his customary
manner, in a straight line, his step springy as modernity itself.
The sky had turned greenish-yellow, what blasphemy was said
to look like once upon a time. Everywhere was evidence of
scholarship: scrolls, cudgels, sacks to tote. In front of the music
building, a dozen students dressed in shimmer stood in a pre-
cise file. They had fierce, determined faces, what kamikazes
were thought to look like, and muttered into their fists. Admissions reported that there were thousands of students now—the
craven and the mighty, fans of one science or another. They
resembled hounds or crawling quadripeds. Some had affiliated
themselves with social clubs, drawn near one another by a
shared interest in bombast or rowdiness. They were cowboys,
memphitites, janissaries. To class, they brought jackstays,
epodes, sporules. They dedicated themselves to epigraphy, to
sponsion, to what inflammation means. In keeping with tradition, Coach Knapp had attended their parties. They celebrated

complexity, nuance. They were the gummata, the kinematic. At the School of Applied Practice, they traveled in groups. One heard them in the early morning, theirs a singsong that had to do with kindredness. In other hours, one heard screech and riot given syntax. They painted their residences to resemble objects of desire and people they'd once loved.

"What is it we subscribe to?" one group was saying now. Their leader was a senior named Don, and around him in a ragged circle sat the females he hunkered with. They believed in tigers burning bright and gnarled trees of mystery.

"Where are we going?" Don hollered.

"Up," was the answer.

Don had a worried-man's face, a creased thing suffused with darkness. Soon he would graduate and toil in the outlands.

"When are we going?"

"Now," they said.

On the steps nearby, uncommonly rigid and sharp-eyed, had gathered the matriculants of the Department of Poesy. Each affected the face of his favorite versifier: Rah, the Sylphides, Lex Luthor. These were to be the next generation of litterateurs, Coach knew. They would produce books, tracts, documents that refuted the accepted wisdom. In the end, another generation would come along. Tricks would be played, points of view offered, positions debated. Scholars would hear of afflatus, disquisitions, stuff in dreadful tongues.

In its way, writing was like football itself: there was contact and joy at the end of it.

. . .

Outside the President's door sat a secretary using the phone. Several things about her—her whichaway hair, her upcast eye-

balls, one hand sawing in the air—said motherhood, a concern
for others.

"Are you listening?" she was saying as Coach Knapp stepped
by her. "First, it appears with green eyes, copper skin, a mouth
tender as a child's. It has horns, fangs, forked appendages. It
sprouts, blossoms, shrivels, has tendrils, converts easily to liquid. It serenades, wheedles, cajoles, barks. Its body is indescrib-
able—features of goat, canine, scale of fish. It's made of dross,
it's made of sputum. It causes a bloody flux."

The President was waiting. He was part Arab, part something else. Oklahoman maybe. Nobody knew. One of seven
cousins who owned the college, he had discovered something
in the Wadi, in the Heights, in the Gulf. It was a process, a
refinement, a radical personal philosophy. Soon there was capi-
tal, assets, plunder, booty. Things were organized and pro-
duced. Titles were conferred. The cousins owned goods,
services, personalities. Their logo—and the team's own
name—was an arrangement of tiny but essential bones that
had to do with longevity.

"I've been thinking about reality," the President said. "Particularly its specifications, the hardware vital to it. It's a big
subject."

The President had a seal's slick hair, as well as the hands and
precious feet of a jazz dancer. He liked to host parties that
involved glee and out-of-body travel.

"Let us stand by the window," the man said. "We can
watch."

Coach Knapp could still hear the secretary in the other
room. "It's under the Ns," she was saying. " 'Nosology,' 'nos-
tic,' 'nostril'—in there somewhere. It ravishes, torments, has
gall. What a marvel it is."

In the distance, half in the shadows of the stadium itself,
Coach Knapp saw his players moving like an army. They car-

ried torches, penlights, smoky kerosene lamps, and they were headed for their dormitory, an exclusive facility that towered over its neighbors. Once inside, they'd prepare themselves. They would review, recapitulate, speculate. Out would go furniture, accoutrements, luxuries; in would come victuals and liquids, what the creature in them cried for. They were men who yearned for that agreement which could be found only in another man's bulky arms.

"I adore these moments," the President remarked.

"As do I," Coach Knapp said.

"Pads, headgear, scurrying in one direction—I am enamoured of the whole thing."

"It is a spirit," Coach said. "Relationships, various coordinations. I'm humbled by the purity of it."

The men stood shoulder to shoulder. Below, on a stubbled, litter-strewn acre known as The Square of Past Mistakes, a pep rally was beginning.

"Still," the President said, "there are issues to guard against."

"One hopes to have a positive effect," Coach Knapp said. "Yet it is seldom the kids say anything to you. There's a barrier, I create it. My people don't call me Woody. My father's people used to call him Moe, and often I think it would be nice to be called Woody, to be friends. But that's not my job. My job is to treat them brutally; theirs, to love it."

From the other room came that voice again, the secretary. " 'Geniculation,' " she was saying, "the state of being geniculate."

Down below, the coach for the other team was being burned in effigy. His people were the Dukes, their mascot the dainty porringer of Count Ugo Malatesta. They were big, it was rumored. Like storybook farm life. And strong. They had one play, Wild Pinch Ollie, which did not involve the ball but

which called upon an underclassman named Ham to lift his
arms and pray in an annoying voice.

"I have the need to reveal myself to you," the President said.
"I can trust you, I feel. I have confessions. At times, I am quite
bad. I am headstrong, for example. I don't know any Greek.
I give money away. Other times, I am surprised by my own
goodness. I am generous to my wives. I like to breed. Ideas
come to me, I scribble them down, attempt to bring them to
fruition. I can make a scarf joint."

"You would have been an excellent weakside linebacker."

"Yes," the President said, "when one dashes off the field,
there shouldn't be anything left."

"It's unfortunate you're not a coach," Woody Knapp said.
"We could study film together, confide in each other. At
halftime, you could stand up and make one hundred youngsters
feel very inadequate."

"I could have been responsible for recruiting, say. Or the
defensive backfield."

"You could show them what the world looks like and why
there is so much screaming."

The fire below was beautiful. In the past, fans had charred
the likenesses of Gator and Bruin. This season they would
incinerate the Schismata, the Tartars. This year the Gentoo,
the hymenopterous insects, the Galbanum—all the disagree-
able, seductive notions they stood for—would go up in flames.
The same songs would be heard, "Tell Me What You Know"
and "All Hail the Power." Insights would be advanced, mean-
ings detailed. Months from now one would have numbers to
measure achievement.

"One more thing, Coach."

"Yes."

"Explain, please, the Strong G Wham."

Woody Knapp's hands fluttered like birds. He described

movements, a frame of reference, what work the heart did. He discussed action in terms of phylum, genre, a specific ligament. He offered metaphor. Deep structure. Deconstruction. Tool and man.

"Check Magoo," he said. "Stem to cover Three. Willie Sam Flop One. The Cat's gotta get into the middle. Up blasts the Monster. Think turnover. Rover has deep responsibility, Red Ryder the underbody. We defoliate and make a Sweep. Then there's the Nether Parts."

"And Little Piggy?"

"Little Piggy stays home."

. . .

Outside, in the twilight, Coach Knapp moved quickly but deliberately. It was one of his precepts. "Pick a place and go to it," he would say. "Conceive and act." All around him, by contrast, wandered the distracted and the aimless. Sport—especially sport that required pain and constant doctoring—would have made everyone more saintly. There were things that could be understood only at the bottom of a mound of flesh. Coming toward him, accelerating like a steam train, charged Lefty Mantillo, the publicist. He was wearing a new outfit now, one of bangles and chrome hasps, his evening dress.

"I'm glad I found you," he said. "I got an inspiration."

Coach Knapp could see a line of lights on the mesa above the valley. Fans, he thought. Like players, they moved in bunches now. They wore red, or black, and had the look of humans who scrambled dawn to dusk. They could not gambol. Neither could they cavort.

"We do a movie," Lefty was saying, "a feature. Super eight, three-quarter tape, noise reduction—the works. We change your mother's name. Serena, Philomel—something with lilt.

We allude to catamites. You moralize, hector. I have ideas for
vistas, soft focus, stop-action, you in the misty twilight, leaves
on the ground, billowy cloudwork. A narrator. Flow and irony.
We loop in the bullshit in post-production."

Coach Knapp was saddened by the image of himself. There
was so much to learn nowadays—where beautiful women came
from, what to make of metaphysics, the subtleties of the shud-
dery arts.

"The first reel's all special effects," Lefty continued. "Birth,
youth, rites of passage. The second, I don't know yet. Hoopla,
maybe. Hurly-burly. Bad things happen. You emerge. Football
enters the current times."

"I like it," Coach said.

"I hums, sahib. It says tie-in, promotion, scratch 'n' sniff. It's
killer material, that's what it is. Contemplative but with the
rough stuff left in."

"I have to go, Lefty."

Mantillo's eyes went out of focus, came back. He hugged
himself as if something—a crucial tissue, a fluid—were about
to spill out.

"Ten-four, Coach. I gotta get back to work. I'm excited, I
tell you. It's like getting aroused. I love this art business."

Coach Knapp ducked around one corner. And another. Direction signs stood up all over, from the folks in Orientation:
ESCHEW GLUTTONY; THE TIMES ARE NEVER SO BAD; GO BACK,
THIS IS NOT FOR YOU. A few people in that department were
former players who held convocations to propose answers to
impossible questions. They quoted Karl Barth, the Wallendas,
seers from the dark atomic years. "Suck it in," they ordered.
"Stand up tall. Don't be a drag-ass."

Now Coach Knapp was aware of someone following him.
There was shambling, a trepidation. Nerve was being sum-

moned. Soon there would be a clearing of the throat. Then speech.

"Who are you?" Coach asked.

Out of the gloom shuffled a figure, something wrought. It was the person in the stands earlier in the afternoon, the one who'd waved.

"I know you," Coach said. "Your name is Griggs. Emile, possibly. You were called the Snake, I believe. This was ages ago. The Lizard. A member of the reptile family."

The man came closer, smiling.

"Height, six-two. Weight, one ninety-six. I never forget these statistics. Your favorite dinner, what you dreamed. You attended school in Cupertino, I remember. Had trouble with world geography."

"Culver," the man said. "It's not there anymore."

Griggs looked like the poorly fitted parts of many other men. His posture said "Assemble with care." It said "Close cover before striking."

"What do you want, Mr. Griggs?"

"Football," he answered. "I want to wear what everyone else does. I want to take directions from somebody named Lance or Butch. I want knowledge alien to the outside world."

A fiber had let go in Coach Knapp, a link to memory. Here was ash, here was dust.

"Are you still fast?"

Griggs raced away, darted back. "I'm fast."

"Are you strong, mean?"

"I could apply myself," Griggs said. "Things could be applied to me."

"What about age?" Coach said. "You must be middle, late thirties."

"I have wisdom," Griggs insisted. "I know things. The fornix, for example. How to foregather, where to look for ground water. I have enthusiasm."

"I could've used you ten years ago."

Griggs edged forward, his posture an underling's.

"You could use me now," he said. "I could be a conduit, a transitor, your voice in the muddle. I could be a moral value. Truth, say. Something vaunted, an idealization. I'd be a whirl-wind."

A noise composed of yowling and shouting had risen in the west. Coach Knapp believed it the cries those in history were famous for. Ideas, in the form of people, were colliding. Bad, or weak, ideas would be seen in the morning like trash on a beach.

"You are staying nearby?" Coach asked.

Griggs nodded. He had a residence. Four stakes in the dirt, a rag to crawl under in the dark.

"Go there," Coach said.

"You'll call for me?"

Coach thought he might.

"I could offer myself elsewhere," Griggs said. "I have a list—opponents, those without scruple. I can't take much more wandering. I thirst, I hunger."

Griggs was moving off, bent and sly, the animal half of him alert and watchful. In the distance, the shrieking had become speech, then prattle again. A concord was being reached, disunion overlooked.

"Griggs?" Coach called. "What's your greatest thrill?"

The man had a smile like daylight.

"To break the plane of the goal line," he yelled back. "I want to vault forward and dance by myself in front of eighty thousand people."

Outside his office, Coach Knapp found Nate Creer interrogating a player. The kid was strapped to a chair, a gooseneck lamp over his head, its light a noontime glare. Around them, on the floor, were scattered groundnuts, alkaloids, an overnight bag. "We've been here a while," Creer explained. The kid was in shock, eyes bulging, sweating.

Nate was name-calling. "Hydroid dipstick, muck-faced fart-breath," he was screaming. "Colewort motherhumper. Salmon slime!"

"What's the problem here?" Coach asked.

"He says he's hurt."

The kid's face went three or four directions.

"I'm hurt," the kid said. "I'm hurt."

"He denies he's a dickweed."

"I deny," the kid blubbered. "I deny."

"He swears on his mother, his father."

The kid's jaw dropped. He swore, he swore.

"What's his story?"

"The usual," Nate began. "Parturition, a time of running about unsupervised, body hair. Hormones, friendship—the years all run together. A succession of pets, an allowance. A world view develops, life becomes complicated. An attitude is adopted. Vocabulary expands, paperwork accumulates. Courtship, a tearful reunion, admissions of guilt. There is commingling, disappointment."

"Then what?"

Nate Greer pounded his fist in exasperation.

"Then this squirrel-faced, rat-eyed squamoid yellow-belly fractures his wrist."

Up went the kid's arm. Knobby and blue, it looked like a peculiarly cunning but soft club.

"I figure an hour more, then I let him go," Nate Creer said. "I got things to say here, a position to defend."

"This is a bad sign, Nate."

The man shrugged. "Bad signs are everywhere, Coach. I tend to ignore them."

In his office, Coach Woody Knapp kept the lights off. The dark had its comforts. It encouraged reflection, maximum self-awareness. It allowed for a summing up, a casting forward. He would be home in an hour. There would be food, badinage. Mrs. Knapp, Helen, would tend to him. All had been done that could be. There would be sleep, morning. Time would shrink, disappear. Then he would be back here again, his people ready, his advice delivered. There would be football then.

And nothing else.

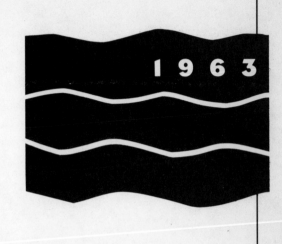

Suddenly, just she remained there, staring at him from the shade of the Mayflower moving van. Then she started toward the porch, where he sat in the old man's aluminum lawn chair, and the clatter in his mind about her halter and shorts and perfect skin was as loud as it could be and still stay there.

She was saying New Mexico was the hottest place on earth, like hell itself, and made a sweep of her arms that took in the Bairds' pea-green house on the corner and the cul-de-sac with the rusted basketball goal at the end, to the irrigation canal beyond the adjacent cottonfield—a gesture that very likely included the Organ Mountains thirty miles away. Beyond was White Sands Proving Grounds, where the old man worked.

"My name's Chappy," he said. "Short for 'Chapman.' It's a family name."

"Ah, Dody's big brother." She had the toothy smile of a

starlet, plus a note in her voice that said there were secrets to her.

"Welcome to Gallagher Street," he said.

Chappy had been reading a too-long article in *Sports Illustrated* about a professional diver named Speedy whose specialty was jumping from a platform, often seventy feet up, into incredibly shallow water. "Someday," Speedy had laughed, "I'm going from one hundred feet into absolutely nothing. Zilch. A dry tank."

"I'm Marcia," she said. "Hogan."

He didn't know how to feel about girls who shook hands; it was awfully formal. She had a man's grip besides. "You can tell a go-getter by two things," his father always claimed, "a sure shake and a shoeshine."

Two Mexicans with greasy hair—they were *chollos,* hoods—had done the sweat work of moving Marcia's family in, but a few times Marcia or her mother, a chunky lady with her hair up in a bandana, rushed out to supervise or scold. One time he heard the mother inside the van yelling, then crying. Afterward, the father, a guy with a Friar Tuck haircut and baggy checked Bermudas, charged out the side door and jumped into a yellow Mercury. He'd sat for five minutes before racing away with a screech.

"Where you from?"

"Jersey," she said. "And White Plains, New York, and San Diego. All over. You with the base?"

"My old man's a major," he said. "In Supply." The light spilling from her hair made him want to grab hold, just feel it wash between his fingers. "What about you?"

"Daddy's with Bell Labs," she said. "Something to do with missiles, I guess. He's not a muckety-muck, though. Don't get the wrong idea."

He found himself asking if she wanted a drink, the heat and

all. A soda maybe. He wasn't sure what Elaine—that's what his mother liked to be called—had in the fridge. Marcia could come in if she wanted.

"Better not," she said. "Mother wouldn't know where I am. She's helpless without me. This move has turned her into a certified bitch."

He couldn't find any Cokes so he poured two jelly glasses of lemonade. The glasses were embarrassing—decals of Bugs Bunny, Porky Pig, Yosemite Sam. No go-getters, those guys.

"How long have you been here?" She was sitting in his chair now, and Chappy felt like a fool standing up.

"Off and on, about fifteen years," he said, watching how she pressed the glass to her neck and cheek. "Every time the old man gets sent overseas, Korea and Germany mostly, we go to Maine. That's where the folks are from. Old Orchard Beach."

"Never heard of it," she said.

"Every time he comes back," he said, "we end up here."

She was looking in the direction the Merc had gone.

"That your old man?"

Her eyes were closed. "My mom and I, we don't get along. She thinks twenty-two-year-olds should be married. She's not satisfied till the whole world's as screwed up as she is."

Chappy said she was lucky actually, coming in the summer. "I mean, in the winter it gets real cold. The dust blows the rest of the time. That's when we came, in a dust storm."

She faced him. "Dody tells me you're a juvenile delinquent, is that true?"

He was thinking about dust—"half of California," the old man had joked, grit in everything, the beds and food—and the cheap Broadway Courts they'd stayed in waiting for housing.

"Breaking and entering, right?"

"Dody told you that?"

"He came over on his bike," she said, "walked up to

Momma and big as you please said, 'Hiya, I'm Dody and I live across the street, I know some multiplication tables, my brother's a breaker and an enterer, Daddy eats halibut, and there ain't no such thing as God.' Mother had a cow."

"My old man wouldn't like that stuff about God."

"Is it true, that you're a felon?"

"No," he said, telling her how, when he was eleven, a gang of kids busted into a ratty house on Calle de Sueños. "It was supposed to be abandoned, but an old lady right out of *Psycho* lived in a back room." He and Richie Behrens had hid behind a chest of drawers when she came screaming out at them, swinging a broom. Later, they sneaked out a window to climb a cottonwood tree next door. "We stayed up there the whole afternoon."

That didn't sound like much to her, she said.

"One of the little kids tattled, and the next day a detective came to the house. He tried to scare us."

Her forehead was covered in sweat. "Did he?"

"Marcia!" The chunky lady was waving a dishcloth at them. "Come home. Your father's on the phone. He wants you."

Chappy wanted to say yes, he had been scared, that this detective named Roby was a bona fide son of a bitch, with tattoos and a badge big as a dinner plate; that he'd been fingerprinted, had his picture taken, and that Elaine was bawling and collapsing against the old man, who just kept threatening to beat the shit out of Chappy when they got home.

"Gotta go," she said, "I'll see you around sometime."

She was halfway across the street before he missed it.

"Hey!" he yelled. "What about the glass?" But he guessed she couldn't hear him and he felt stupid hollering about Daffy Duck in the middle of the afternoon.

.   .   .

The guy Dave Garroway was interviewing on TV had a Dick Tracy jaw and a smile like a bad bright light. The man was a loony, yammering about the Russians and ICBMs, plutonium and throw weights per lift/pound of blah-blah-blah.

"This is the scene," the guy was saying, straining forward in his chair, sweat at his hairline, "the communists have dropped the big one—fifty-megaton, say—and you're in your fallout shelter, well-stocked and so forth, and your neighbor, a man you've known for ten years, well, he wants in too. He has his family out there, they're wailing like banshees. But they're contaminated, Dave. They dripping with it."

The man shook himself, genuinely frightened about the idea of radioactive dust on his shoulders.

"This guy's talking golf and canasta and trips to Mission Beach. He's talking friendship and decency and respect. And his skin is melting! What are you going to do? Let him in?"

Chappy switched off the set after Garroway asked the man what he'd do.

"Blow them up," he said. "I've got a Remington twelve-gauge. No choice, it's him or me."

In the bathroom Chappy found a note taped to the mirror. *Dody and I went with your father to work. We'll be at the PX, then the Officer's Club. Don't waste your time on the people across the street. They're snobs. Elaine.*

It was only eleven when he got outside, but already hot. The light, pink and coming from eight million places at once, made the buildings look crooked and insubstantial—the way they were in dreamland—and it hurt his eyes to concentrate. The moving van was gone. So was the Merc. Different curtains hung in the windows. The front door looked strange, too, but he couldn't figure out why. Painted probably.

"Hey, Speedy!" Marcia stood near the basketball goal at the dead end down the street. She handled the ball awkwardly, like a shot put, no balance, making a loud "Ooommpphh" each time she threw it up.

He felt sorry for girls who played sports, always bending wrong and making the same mistake again and again. They seemed desperate and self-conscious, all elbows and flying legs, and he wondered what they were trying to prove. "I didn't know you played."

"There's a lot you don't know," she said, trying to dribble. The ball squirted between her legs and he grabbed it. "I'm not very good, right?"

He'd played in junior high, the C team, guard. The coach— a lumpy idiot named Mirmanian—sent him on the court only when the game was out of reach. Way out of reach. Chappy could still hear Coach blowing his whistle and screaming during drills. "Hustle, you punk. Dig, dig, dig. Who you think you are, Cousy?" Then he'd whistle to the A and B teams, mostly black kids and Mexicans, scrimmaging at the other basket. "Hey, boys, say howdy to Bob Cousy. Show us your moves, Bobby!"

"You know what I've been?" Marcia was saying. "I've checked groceries at a Piggly Wiggly, been a secretary to a justice of the peace. I know a little something about trucking regulations, don't ask me how, and I've car-hopped. My mother says I'm going nowhere fast. My dad thinks I'm a princess, can do no wrong."

Chappy found himself wishing he had Mirmanian's silver whistle. That or a twelve-gauge. Do some blowing up one day.

"You have a girlfriend, Chappy?"

He leaned against the goalpost. "I'm playing the field."

She didn't believe him, and the way her eyes met his— steady but empty as buckets, as if she knew everything there was to know about him—encouraged him to tell the truth.

"I don't go out much." He liked the way she sat. "Not

a lot to do here. Go to the drive-in. The flumes, now and then."

"What's that?"

"It's a viaduct that crosses the Rio Grande. You can jump from it into the river."

"You ought to take me out there sometime."

It was usually crowded, he said, but sure, they'd go out there. She seemed strong, no flab, real muscles in her thighs and calves, none of that chicken skin under the arms.

"You ever been in love, Chappy?"

He could hear something in the question he didn't like, a part you could hurt yourself on.

"I don't think so," he told her.

"Not even a little bit?"

He felt like the guy on Garroway's show—an adult from Hamtramck, Michigan, so wrought up with worry over the end of the world he didn't know what to do with his arms and his legs in the here and now.

"What was her name?"

"Pat," he said, wishing he hadn't spoken so fast. "Patricia, actually. Greathouse. Her father worked with the FBI. We don't go out anymore."

"And you still love her, right?"

Some feeling came back to him then, and he said, "No, she's a snob."

. . . .

That afternoon, in bed, Chappy's mind was drawn up tight, reimagining the Shaffer twins—Bonnie and Connie.

They were beautiful: thick black hair, the sharp features of beach girls in Malibu movies, plus classy figures. They had reputations for being fast and once he'd gone out with one of them. Connie, he thought it was. Their father operated a construction outfit out of their house, and Chappy remembered their horseshoe drive next to a lot filled with backhoes and, like teacups from Wonderland, cast concrete cesspools. When he rang the bell, both girls answered. Did Connie want to go out, he asked, and the one on the right—the one whose moving parts were all creamy and loose—said why not.

At the Rocket Drive-In, they sat in the backseat necking. Once he felt her breast, which was firm and larger than he expected. She could French-inhale, sit in a yoga position, thought Kennedy was cool. When he learned she wasn't wearing any underwear—she'd pulled his hand between her legs— he took her home.

"We'll go out again sometime," the girl had said. "You're a real gentleman." Afterward, he drove Highway 85 to its intersection with the Rio Grande, then followed the levee road to the flumes. The water ran so shiny and black he thought he might jump in—clothes, shoes, wallet, watch, the works.

"Chappy?" Dody stood at the foot of the bed, wearing a leatherette holster with one cap-gun. "How old are you?"

"Who wants to know?"

Dody pointed outdoors. Marcia.

"Tell her I'm twenty." It was a good age—full of promise. "She send you in here?"

"Nobody sends me anywhere, mister."

Chappy heard him racing down the hall, the front door banging, and then Dody yelling, "He's eighteen." And then maybe he heard a girl's sigh of disappointment, but he wasn't sure. It could have been his imagination.

It was the room, he figured, that made Dody such a smart-aleck. Elaine called it their environment—brown chenille bedspreads with embroidered ranch brands and coiled lariats, bucking broncos and ten-gallon hats on the matching curtains.

On the walls hung drawings of hot rods and Army pictures of Nike missiles that they'd gotten from Grumman. Over Dody's bed hung a pair of gold-painted plaster-of-Paris hands clasped in prayer.

The sky was a huge white sheet and his head felt impossibly heavy. The whole neighborhood was out—the Geists, the Aldoms, even Mr. and Mrs. Odom, J.E. and Vi. They had given Chappy the plaster hands. They were always pestering him to go to MYF at their church. He went once, but everyone was so big-hearted he felt like an orphan. Or a deaf-mute. He remembered sitting across from a preacher who said "cool" and "man" a lot, and then eating tuna casserole topped with crushed potato chips. It tasted like dust. California dust.

"I had a car once," Marcia said. Using a bucket of soapy water, she was washing the Merc on her lawn. The old man always said soap took the wax off. No soap. Ever. "A Ford Fairlane 500. Black over white. Automatic transmission. A real dream."

He had something to tell her, he understood now. A true thing involving one Shaffer twin. And if Marcia would look at him, he would say it.

"I wrecked that car." Marcia sprayed the hood with the hose. "Drove off a freeway in Rochester—failure to use due care. Seventy miles an hour and—boom!—instant junk."

Dorcey Wingo's father had a car like hers—AM-FM radio, power windows, whitewalls you could use shoe polish on—and once Chappy and Dorcey had gone cruising in it, back and forth between Heibert's and Jerry's Bar-B-Que, Betsy Aldom and Nell Jean Sanders riding along. Two months later, last October, Dorcey joined the Army. "I'm getting all the nooky in Georgia," he'd written. "Join up, buddy. The South's the place for us!"

"You doing anything tonight?"

There is water, he thought. And sunlight, and grass, and there is something to say.

"Daddy's taking us out," she told him. "What about tomorrow?"

That was fine. But there was more, the sloppy weight of it pounding here and there in his chest. About himself. About preachers and missiles and tin cap-guns. About what she and he were going to be to each other.

"My treat," she was saying. "Money is no problem." She grabbed the chamois and slapped it on the hood. "Want to help?"

He was watching water soaking his cuffs. "Marcia, I'm not a virgin, okay?"

    . . .

He drove her the length of Main, pointing out where the Thunderbird Bowling Alley burned down and the barbershop where he used to get his hair cut. "I'm letting it grow out now," he said. "I had a flat-top." Cars shot by, honked. He thought he saw Pat Greathouse's Impala, but he couldn't be certain. Too many girls and the one behind the wheel had blonde hair, not brown.

The movie stank—the sound was garbled, the screen wrinkled—and the film broke twice, which made the plot like algebra to follow, but Marcia said not to worry, it was nice just being out. "You're all right, Chappy," she said, but in the light from the screen she looked eerie and semi-evil.

Three different movies seemed to be playing at the same time—all featuring the same man and woman. The woman was always laughing at the man and shoving his face in a grapefruit, later a chocolate pie. A swinging door smashed him in the nose.

A poodle ripped his dress pants. He stumbled into an empty swimming pool and twice a seedy guy in a Hopalong Cassidy hat clobbered him in the ear. "This is the pits," Marcia said.

Chappy said they could leave if she wanted.

"So why don't you take me to the flumes?"

The short way—through Dona Ana, Les Fletcher's pig farm and the abandoned Mennonite orphanage—took them past acres and acres of pecan groves and onion fields. One summer he'd chopped cotton in this area, cutting out weeds with a hoe, his companion a Polish kid named Ears whose uncle owned the farm. "I'm quits," Ears always said at about two, when the sun beat down like a sledge. "I'm going into town." Once he returned with a girl and they sat in the pickup, watching Chappy trudge up and down the furrows until five. "This is Linda," Ears said. Chappy wiped his face with his shirttail, thought he recognized her. Just then she stood up and stripped off her blouse. Ears, laughing hard ("Jesus," Ears said later, "it was only a joke"), almost tumbled out of the truck when she held up her naked breasts and said, "Eat your heart out."

"The first time," Marcia was saying, "I did it right. A motel, clean sheets, a bottle of Cold Duck."

The last Chappy heard, Ears was living in a trailer park in Brownfield, Texas. He didn't know what happened to the girl.

"His name was Buddy," Marcia said. "He had hair all over, not just the chest. But down the back, on his shoulders. A real gorilla. I went with him a year almost, after I graduated. He wasn't tough at all."

Chappy asked about love, was there any of that.

"I loved them all," she said. "I got a weakness for weird guys. My mother says I collect losers."

They were on the levee road, gravel banging the undercarriage of the car.

"There was a bunch," she said. There was an Edward who

worked as a proofreader for a law office in Redlands, and a Thomas not a Tom who sold ads for a weekly newspaper, and a bartender named Mike who taught her how to make Brandy Separators, and a second Mike who didn't do anything special.

"In here." Chappy pointed to the road that ran onto the floodplain underneath the trestle to the viaduct. The place was deserted. And dark.

"When I was a little girl," Marcia was saying, "I thought I was the center of the whole world. Whatever I wanted would be mine. I had a lot of love in me then."

"What did you want?"

But the car was already stopped and she was out of the door, heading toward the ladder that went up the trestle. "Where do I jump?" she hollered.

Watching her cat-walk the ironworks over the river, Chappy supposed he had a lot of love in him too. Love went at high speed, or not at all. It shrank or bent time, made objects move or disappear. It had a smile and eight ways of saying hello, and when it stopped, you felt like a dufus for believing it. "There's a spot in the middle," he told her. If she went in feetfirst, she wouldn't get hurt.

"What about your clothes?" he shouted.

"I'm taking them off."

After each dive, she crawled out on the opposite bank and climbed the trestle from the other end. Chappy could barely see her—just a falling white blur, shrieking that the water was cold, the current weak. The first time she yelled "Geronimo!" and plunged in headfirst, a dive fifty percent swanlike and mostly terrible. She stayed under a long time, but when he started to worry that she'd snapped her neck, she burst to the surface, shaking like a wet dog. "Fooled you," she cried.

Before the third dive, she sat, knees pulled to her chin, a mile or two of river sloshing by.

"What're you doing?" he said.

Her answer, muffled and partly unhappy, came from a long way off: "Thinking."

"About what?"

A funny, choked laugh, then: "Gorillas."

Later a car drove up, its headlights catching Marcia standing on the concrete pylon. She was incredibly white—like paper, like icing—and Chappy felt himself freeze inside, link after link after link: there was her, and him, and danger that might not ever go away. The lights blinked to high beam, but she didn't cover herself or turn her back. Her hands at her sides like a librarian, she glared, shaking her head, her frown one pleasure Chappy was proud of. After the car went dark, a lot of noise came from inside; then the lights flashed on again, the horn blasting, and the car, a Chevy, backed up in a fury.

"Friends of yours?" she called. "Little high school boys?"

He didn't know, but for a moment he thought of Edward and Thomas not Tom and the Two Mikes—guys he wouldn't want to meet.

All the way home she kept brushing her hair to dry. Once she stuck her head out the window and yelled, but the wind sucked the words away so all he caught was her tone—angry, as if she were about to do something she'd promised never to do again.

"Stop here," she said at his house. Then she grabbed him. She was cold and smelled like rusty, muddy water, and he wasn't sure how to hold her, so he squeezed with his elbows, his hands silly and useless and empty. She kissed his neck, lightly at first but harder when he forgot to breathe—as if she had something to prove. Her lips were dry and rough, and when he felt her tongue against his teeth like a new knife, something—a bone or a muscle that stretched the length of him—snapped free.

"Chappy," she said, before letting him go. "Definitely not a Chapman."

.   .   .

That night the ghosts rose up in dreamland to hold his hand and sit across from him. Barbara Camunez forgave him for spying on her through the hole in the Sanderses' bathhouse and for the clumsy, chlorinated French kiss he tried in the deep end of the pool. Kay Stevenson, the freeze-tag queen, followed. She had nothing to feel sorry for, she was so young then. He was young too. And Billie Jean Maxwell, his first steady, sixth grade, and only because Michelle Parker and Mark Runyan were doing it did she allow Chappy to explore the spots on her where one day she would have parts she might not let him touch again.

All through the night they rose up and disappeared:

Ruby Levisay, a tall creature he couldn't walk next to without stumbling.

Mrs. Sutherland, fifth-period English last year, Shakespeare and Milton and the stockings she had.

Rodeo champion Betty Greene, throwing hay bales, eyes like a lizard.

And Greathouse, Patricia. He dreamed her as clearly as if they were again lying on Dick and Joe Anderson's sofa, Mr. and Mrs. Anderson gone overnight to Albuquerque. He saw her slamming against him—dry-humping—and the hi-fi playing Buddy Holly and the Platters, the "Great Pretender" lyrics digging to the dry center of him. And in the deep distance, beyond the low lights, beyond the Colony Garden apartments themselves, at the crossroads of memory and desire, he saw, lounging in the cup of a cast cesspool, the twins, Bonnie and Connie.

"I lied," he said to Marcia that morning. She stood inside her screen door, a shadow he could talk to.

"You can't come in," she said. "I mean, nobody's home. This is a really shitty day, Chappy. The folks are fighting again."

He couldn't see much—Mexican ceramic plates and a wall mirror—but he had the feeling of heaviness: oversize furniture—what was had in a giant's world—dark woods, and carpet you'd hate to vacuum. Not like Elaine's. No cut glass or silver or hand-painted bone china or miniature tea services or antique flatirons used as planters.

"Are you sick?" he asked.

Her hand at her forehead, she said no. "I'm mad at the world, okay? I get mad easily, make scenes. You'll learn that about me."

Except for Chappy nobody was outdoors, and all the houses seemed closed up, as if the whole block had vanished. The only sound was Marcia's picking at the screen, and Chappy remembered how, only hours ago, she had come at him from three directions at once.

"I lied," he said. "I've never been with a girl."

She held the iron grillwork on the inside of the screen.

"I've been to Juarez a few times. The White Lakes, Cherry Hill—those places. I didn't have the guts."

He ordered himself to slow down, to take his hands out of his pockets, to stand up straight. He was going to college in two months, he was going to be something. An engineer. A pilot.

"Harry Hansen took me to El Paso once," he said. He told her how he ended up with a Del Norte High School girl—maybe she was eighteen—who owned a green Caddy. She had a fifth of Bacardi and they drove, raced actually, for hours before she took him to her place near the old country club. They sat outside for a long time, Chappy in a creaky hammock.

Then she unbuttoned his shirt. "I didn't know what to do,"
he said.

Marcia pulled back, took with her a lot of sunlight and air.
"I just let her pick at me, this blonde girl."

She asked what happened, what the end of the story was.

"I blacked out," Chappy said. "Next thing I know, I'm
sitting in Harry's car, we're on the highway, and he's beating
the dashboard with his fist, screaming, 'Wasn't it great!
Wasn't it the goddamn greatest!' We're weaving all over, he's
jumping up and down at the wheel, and I'm scared. Jesus."

For a second, he wasn't sure Marcia was there any longer,
and it occurred to him that he was still asleep.

"Chappy?"

He tried backing up, but his feet wouldn't move.

"I lied too," she said.

He braced himself, tightened his stomach, waited for her to
tell him to get lost.

"I never owned a car," she said. "That Fairlane belonged to
a jerk I used to sleep with. You don't want to know the details."

After she closed the door, he held an inventory of himself:
a wild pulse beating in his eyes, breath whooshing in and out
of him like a wet wind, and one thought he had no English for.

. . .

Marcia's father sat on the fender of the Merc, smoking. He was
wearing his Bermudas again, a dingy shirt, a Sam Snead golf
hat, and GI cloth slippers with WBGH stenciled in black on
the toes. He'd called Chappy over, had something to tell him.
Dody was there, too, straddling his bike and trying to be important.

"You want to see pain?" Evidently, Mr. Hogan once had a
solid build, but now his stomach hung over his belt—like Dory

Funk, Sr., Channel 5's favorite wrestler—and the flesh on his
arms looked stretched and weak. "I'll show you pain," he said,
yanking off his shirt.

Chappy thought Marcia was inside. He could feel her somewhere.

"See this?" The ragged scar ran from his breastbone down
his chest to below his ribs and continued on his back, parallel
to the spine, finishing beneath the shoulder blade. The new
tissue was yellow—like the Merc.

"Hemorrhoids," he said, laughing.

Dody stood next to him, openmouthed.

"Admitted for hemorrhoids," Mr. Hogan was saying, "they
find a black spot on a lung during X ray and—Boom!—out
comes a handful. A hundred eighty-six stitches. That's pain."

"Christ on a crutch," said Dody.

"Tubes coming out of me everywhere." He spit on the
grass. "Mouth, nose, side, gut, pecker—hell, I looked like a
Tennessee still. Three months, they had me, for crying out
loud."

"Crap," Dody was saying.

He'd done and been a lot of things, he said. He'd pole-
vaulted cross-handed—"cleared eleven feet and then some!"—
and lost a sister in a drowning accident and a brother in Bataan,
and the other brother worked for a finance company, and he'd
played a round of golf with Dr. Cary Middlecoff—"beat him,
too!"—and for a quarter he'd danced to Count Basie and the
Dorsey Brothers years and years ago; his wife was Canadian
and, Lord Almighty, he'd raised one hell of a fine-looking
daughter.

"Like a still," Chappy heard behind him. It was Dody, shirt
up and pants at his knees, pointing out to another kid the spots
Mr. Hogan had talked about. "Nose, side, gut, pecker."

"No way," the kid was saying.

"Here." A ten-dollar bill was in the man's hand. "Take her someplace nice, huh? She likes you. You remind her of somebody, she says."

And then, in the moment Mr. Hogan shooed Dody away, a key appeared and fell into Chappy's hand.

"Use the Merc," he said, and the bill went in Chappy's shirt pocket. "Enjoy yourself. I want her to be happy."

Chappy didn't move until Mr. Hogan disappeared inside and Dody was down the block with his pal. And then, in the middle of the street, he stopped, thinking he heard the man yelling. "Hunky-dory," he was shouting. "That's just fucking hunky-dory with me!"

.   .   .

She stormed out of the house wearing dark slacks and a south-of-the-border blouse he'd seen only on actresses, ruffles at the neck and cuffs, and when she got in the car he saw she was wearing lipstick he thought might taste like salt.

"Listen, I'm sorry," he said, aiming to say more, but she slammed the door. It wouldn't stay shut so she slammed it again. And again. And again.

"Please, please, please," she said, pulling the door closed slowly, speaking as if it were a kid, saying it could be good, if it wanted, if it tried, there was nothing easier than being decent to someone.

"Let's go, champ," she said.

Out of habit he turned onto Alameda, and it wasn't until they passed the Little Store where he'd bought ice cream and Dr Peppers as a kid that he asked, "Where?"

They were driving past houses that dated from the twenties and thirties, bigger and more ramshackle than his, three-story piles with white pillars and wood shingles and massive hedges.

"It's the money," Chappy said. "I didn't want to hurt his feelings, that's all."

They drove until the streetlights switched on, past Court Junior High and the downtown Women's Club and Atlas Lumber, where he worked the summer before as a shipping clerk.

"Don't be angry, okay? He was—"

"Just drive," she said. "I'll do the thinking."

They were heading west, toward the line that was sunset above the mesa—orange upon red upon gold, until it was black high up and forever—past the American Legion ballpark with the green bleachers (he'd played Pee-Wee League there) and Ace Hardware, and a couple of auto repair shops, and the Del Norte Motel, where he swam before the old man joined the country club. The only time she moved was to turn the radio to a cowboy station, and for a few blocks they listened to what a Texas shitkicker thought was poetic about moonlight and cheek-to-cheek do-si-do.

"Stop here," she said.

The Neff Motel ("Kitchenettes") was small, but each room had its own carport. Beside the pool (nobody in it), which was surrounded by a chain-link fence, sat a swing set with a slide and four plastic pink flamingoes that stood on one leg and were intended to look tropical. Chappy thought he'd heard the old man say that Neff and his wife had sold out, gone to Korea. Philippines maybe. They were missionaries, Mormons or the like, who endeavored to serve God in the boondocks.

"Wait," she said.

At the little house that was the lobby and registration desk, she tried the door, then knocked, not moving until a man wearing khaki slacks and bathrobe over his T-shirt let her in.

"Wait," she had said. "I'll do the thinking," she'd said.

She used three cards signing in—"Please, please," Chappy

thought she might be telling herself, "be nice"—ripping two in half and jamming the pieces in her pocket before paying.

"Follow me."

Because his hands didn't work and four thoughts were banging this way and that, Chappy pressed the accelerator too hard and almost hit her. If he weren't in Mr. Hogan's car, he knew he'd feel better. He wanted to run but didn't know where. The ballpark, maybe. Sit in the bleachers. Maybe the Philippines.

"Follow me," she had said.

The room, number 8, smelled of wintergreen, wax and dust. The carpet looked as if a whole race of salesmen and truckers had walked across it, each one standing for hours in front of the mirror, his eyes flat and defeated.

"Marcia," he said. Water gurgled in the bathroom.

The pink walls had smudges above the headboard, and he heard music somewhere—metallic and heavy. There had been pictures, he thought, but he couldn't imagine what of.

When the water in the toilet stopped running, he noticed the bedspread was almost like his—same thin fabric, same silly fenceposts and barbed wire, same brands. Triple R.

"Do you love me?"

She stood naked, hands behind her back, heels together, a harsh light racing at him from her sockets and pores and teeth.

"Tell me you love me a little. That's all you have to do."

He thought someone was behind him—the gent in the bathrobe maybe—but he was afraid to turn around.

"Jesus," she said, "answer the question."

He might say no, he thought. He might say he'd spent days thinking about it, wishing for it, needing it. But a second passed, long enough for the floor and walls to tilt, and he had said yes.

"That's great," she muttered. She had pulled back the bed-

covers and he saw more of that light which had sound and
smell and touch to it. "That's really hunky-dory."

The whole time he took off his clothes he felt numb and
stupid. And old. So old he couldn't get his zipper down or his
shoes unlaced. Or his belt unbuckled. And when he fumbled
with his shirt buttons, she laughed.

"Hurry up," she said.

He touched her breasts, trying to force out of his mind the
radio going next door.

"Isn't it great," she said, Harry Hansen's words but none of
the joy. "Isn't this goddamn great."

Her lips tasted like wood.

Stolen for a third time, the radio said. *Hit across the—*

Chappy could feel himself coming apart, the wheels and
springs and gadgets of him popping loose and rattling to the
flat bottom of him.

"Why are you doing this?" he said.

She was gazing a point in space near the ceiling.

"I hit a girl once," he began. There was a mile at least
between himself and the kid talking. "In grade school, this girl
wouldn't let me in the door and I kept telling her to open up
or I'd punch her. But she just stood behind the glass, grinning
like crazy, so I smacked her. Through the glass."

The radio reported how life was elsewhere. In Paris, France.
In Peru.

"What if I hit you?" Marcia said.

Two things happened: the words didn't fit right; and when
they did, she had slapped him, not hard, on the cheek.

"Don't, Marcia," he said.

She hit him again, harder, and this time his face stung.

"Stop it," he said.

He jumped off the bed, but she kept coming, flailing at his

face, catching him on the ear, the forearm, the back of the neck. The blows hurt—she meant them to—but all he was thinking about was how little pain he'd felt when he'd crashed his fist through that plate glass years ago.

"You're a real chicken-shit, aren't you?"

Marcia had him backed against the chest of drawers. She didn't look as if she were crying, but there were tears on her cheeks and her nose was red. She slapped him twice more before making a no-account fist to sock him in the belly.

"Please," he said. He grabbed her hands, but she twisted and slipped loose. "Geronimo," she said, the word she'd used at the flumes, but this time there was nothing in it that sounded like fun.

"Marcia, let's go home, okay?"

"Hit me, Chappy." She held her face up, eyes closed. "Don't be afraid, Chapman. You don't want to hurt someone's feelings, do you? You wouldn't want me to be mad, would you?"

When she slugged him on the breastbone, he was thinking about love, the come and go of it, where it would lead you if you weren't careful.

"I feel sorry for you," she said.

He made his fist then, tight, thumb outside the knuckles, the way the old man taught, but when he was ready to swing, she was gone, and it was then that all the pain from the fourth grade hit him. That girl behind the glass had been Ears's girlfriend: Linda. The person in the pickup who'd said something cruel about his heart.

· · ·

Chappy's old man was riding his high horse again. He was talking from the shower, saying Khrushchev was a triple-A bozo. "An asshole," he declared. The old man had other words, too: dipstick, motherfucker, son of a bitch. When he got worked up, these were the only words he knew.

"Can I go now?" Chappy asked.

The old man had a method for taking a shower. He insisted that everyone follow it, including Dody. "One," he'd say, "don't touch the nozzle. Two, seal the curtain against the tile. Three, no wasting time. In and out. Fourth, dry off in the bathroom, I don't want any footprints in the hall. Fifth, hang up the towels, wet on the bottom rack, dry on top."

Now he was getting ready to go to the Giests for a party. Somebody had turned fifty.

"If I get drunk enough," he was saying, "I'll drive home backwards. That makes your mother crazy."

His parents liked to drink, particularly Elaine. Once Chappy found her in the living room, hurling chicken bones at the clock above the desk. Dody was chasing them and keeping score. "Bull's-eye," he shouted every time she struck the clock face and the chimes rang.

When the major got drunk, he'd sit in his chair in the TV room and tell how the chinks in Korea used to steal him blind, making off with—"This is the Lord's truth," he'd say, "I kid you not!"—tanks, flamethrowers, and goddamn truckloads of bazookas. Above the TV hung a charcoal caricature of the major done by a Pusan street artist. He wore a field hat, in his hand a miniature bomb, while behind him, in formation, flew a cloud of B-52s. Still farther behind, at ground level, huddled a group of humanlike specks. Chinks, Chappy used to think. Stealing the old man's goodies.

"The Hogans will be there," he said. "Bert works with the father."

Chappy made his mind, one threadlike nerve at a time, go from Khrushchev to Bert Hogan and back again.

"You want to come along? What's-her-name will be there."

"Marcia?"

The old man stuck his head out, his gray face glazed with water. "Nice, huh?"

"Okay if I stay home?"

The old man said sure, whatever Chappy did was dandy with him.

In a half-hour they were gone, driving away in the olive-green staff car the major took to work. Chappy made Dody take a bath, then go to bed.

"Why?" he whined. "Elaine said I could stay up."

Chappy made a fist and Dody took off, slamming and locking their bedroom door. "Asshole," he yelled. "Dipstick."

Chappy knew what he'd do as soon as *Ed Sullivan* was over, as soon as what Ed thought of as amusing or daring or useful to know was danced and sung or made ridiculous; and so Chappy sat, took note of the sequins and the fat folks and the ha-ha-has. He broke the hour into minutes, and those into heartbeats, and tried to place beyond memory and care the image of Marcia in her underwear, telling him what a coward he was. He thought of himself on TV, all the skinny height of him, and wondered how Ed might introduce him to America. "For I'm a jolly good fellow," he said when the program ended. "Which nobody can deny."

Marcia's house, except for a light in the kitchen, was dark; and when he went in, he promised himself that tomorrow—or the next day, or one fine day after that—he'd tell the Hogans about the nasty characters who sometimes came to their neighborhood.

The kitchen wallpaper had a cornflower design—damned stupid for a desert town. The cabinets looked recently wood-stained, with black iron door and drawer handles: a decor that might impress Elaine. Above the stove was a grease stain and

a singsongy poem about housework, the respect and love that
were its halves. On the sideboard sat dirty dishes—too many
for only the three of them—plus a saucepan of tomato soup
Chappy thought he might eat if he got hungry.

In the living room he lay on a sofa that was too blocky and
uncomfortable. The *Sun News* lay opened to the classifieds;
everybody needed busboys, it seemed. Guys to lift stuff. Mr.
Hogan's bathrobe hung on one chair. Chappy felt almost swal-
lowed when he put it on, the sleeves swinging well past his
hands. On the coffee table, beside a punch bowl full of letters
and cards, a liquor bottle in the shape of a 1 wood was almost
empty—it was scotch, he thought—and on an end table he
found two cartons of Lucky Strikes. He took a pack, lit one,
and went from room to room smoking, no lies in mind about
what he'd say if the Hogans came home now.

In their bedroom he went through their bureaus, examining
each drawer like a detective. He found a handful of silver
dollars and golf tees, stuff they wouldn't miss if he snatched it.
Mr. Hogan had too many undershirts, and boxer shorts. The
windows were covered with venetian blinds and the white
sheer curtains Elaine wouldn't put up with for a second. A
reading light was over the bed, and Chappy tried to imagine
Mr. Hogan lying there, his scar yellow and almost black. In
Mrs. Hogan's chest, he found a whole drawer with nothing but
panties in it—all white, and large enough that two women
could get in them easily. He was a machine, he thought. A
walking, talking contraption of greased joints and complicated
dials; he was an it that clomped and hissed and once or twice
wobbled to a halt.

Chappy spent a long time looking at Marcia's door before
he knocked, two thumps which in the darkness sounded like
faraway thunder. He found perfume—White Shoulders and
Imprévu—the sticky, close smells that made him feel good

about being male. The walls were almost completely covered
with posters and photographs: Roman Gabriel in a Rams uniform; Presley with his hips going whichaway; her own self in
a graduation gown, tassel dangling over one ear. From her
jewelry box, he picked out a charm bracelet and a pair of men's
cuff links. He felt nothing inside—this isn't me, he thought,
this isn't anyone—when he sat on her too-springy bed. He had
the idea that she slept curled. Maybe in a T-shirt. Then he took
the bathrobe and placed it on the spread—"Jesus, it's only a
joke," he heard himself saying—arranging the sleeves like
crossed arms, even knotting the belt, and gave himself five
minutes before he picked up her lipstick to scribble on the
mirror.

. . .

Even from his room Chappy could plainly hear the alarm in
Mrs. Hogan's, Beverly's, voice at the door.

"Marcia's not here?"

"No," Elaine was telling her. "Something wrong?"

"I sent her to the store an hour ago. I thought"—there was
a pause in which anything could have been said—"your boy
might have gone with her."

Chappy heard the squeak of the screen door and his mother
outside saying no, he was in his bedroom asleep probably, that's
all he ever did, kill time and mope around. Then their voices
grew fainter, as if they were moving away from the house, and
finally Chappy heard only the rattle and wheeze of the air
conditioner.

He got to thirty-Mississippi before he heard Elaine back in
the kitchen.

"Your father's going to be late, so it's pretty much catch-as-
catch-can." She had a book he hadn't seen before, the kind she

always read: vaguely indecent, about incest or interracial love, something she got from her sister. Last winter, he'd picked up one—a fat novel about red-dirt Georgia, he thought—and saw that she'd written in the margins the words and foreign phrases she meant to check in the dictionary. All her *m*s and *n*s were upside down, her penmanship as strange as what they had in Arabia.

"I'm going out," he told her.

"If you see Dody, tell him to get his butt home. I'm mad."

Chappy drove the Plymouth down to the Aldoms' before he spotted Dody. He was pitching rocks at a stop sign.

"Marcia's at the Little Store."

"Go home," Chappy said. "Where's your bike?"

"Don't know," he said. "Some creep stole it."

Chappy made sure Dody was on his way home, then turned onto Alameda Street. The sky was a huge gray canopy and many of the clouds, those that looked important or half of a storm, had all the sense of his mother's upside-down letters; if he wanted, he could read the clouds and learn what was being told to him and the ten thousand others hereabouts.

"Get in," he said. "I'll give you a ride."

She sat on the steps of the store, a bag of groceries—a loaf of bread was sticking out—beside her knees. She was wearing a loose dress he hadn't seen before, and green shower thongs. "You just don't know when to quit, do you?"

"Your mother's looking for you."

She put the sack between them and climbed in. "It was you, wasn't it? The mirror."

The emotions came in waves, some having to do with being mighty and rising above, and for a moment he forgot he was driving an unimpressive Plymouth, seeing himself at the wheel of Mr. Hogan's smooth Mercury, steering with his pinky, the whole world stretched out flat and pure.

"You're taking me to the motel, aren't you?"

This time he went in, but instead of the guy with the robe and T-shirt, there was a girl with red hair nobody he knew would want to touch.

"Where's the old guy?" he asked.

"On vacation," she said, news she clearly felt stingy about giving. "Vegas, I think."

Chappy paid, using Mr. Hogan's ten bucks. He couldn't have number 8 because two ladies from Arizona were in it, but 9 was free, if that was all right.

"Dandy," he said.

No radio was playing this time, but he imagined he could hear the two women next door laughing. One voice was low and raspy, the other girlish and a little pained; and when Chappy latched the door chain, he heard the word "stop" as if it had been whispered in his ear.

"One," he said to Marcia, "take off your clothes." He tried to flatten all the terror out of his voice. "Two, sit on the bed. Three, don't hit me again. Ever."

"You don't have to threaten me," she said.

When he put his arms around her, the noise next door stopped. She smelled sweet, soapy, and this time her lips seemed smooth and glassy. He kissed her closed eyes, her temples and her earlobes. A heat came from her skin and one vein on her neck beat slowly. He wanted to be everywhere at once—her shoulder, that nick on her shin, that cherry mole on her neck—but when he heard her breathe, he realized he was nowhere.

"I'm letting you do this," she said. "Screwing doesn't mean anything."

The whole time he lay on top of her, images came and went, pictures that whooshed by at a million miles an hour. He saw himself in the backseat of the major's car with Connie Shaffer, only he wasn't frightened when she grabbed his hand and guided it between her legs. He saw himself with a headful of hair, like the Beach Boys, and new clothes and a car that made a growl you could hear five blocks away. He saw Patricia Greathouse and a swim meet he once won, and in one picture he had a wallet full of cash and three fancy places to spend it. He moved against Marcia and when he was nearly finished, he thought maybe he'd learned something about himself, what hooks and hasps he was and how they fit the thing he aimed to be. Then Marcia touched his ear, and he heard himself splinter like a mirror, and the pictures went as black as the corners of the universe no one would ever reach.

He rolled over and the noises in the adjacent room began again, two voices in argument. On the ceiling was a water stain, yellow and brown, and it took him five beats before he saw in it the shape of a red-bellied man, feeble and goggle-eyed and afraid, now tumbling from a platform high as heaven into nothing at all.

"You can take me home now."

They rode in silence, Marcia clutching the grocery sack and looking straight ahead.

"I don't think you ought to come over anymore," she said.

There were no lights on in his house when he pulled into the drive. "One question," he said. He held the door so she couldn't get out. "Where's the bike?"

Her eyes looked as they did the night he took her to the movies—spooky and not something you'd care to see in daylight. "In the irrigation ditch. I threw it in."

Then he let her go home.

.   .   .

All he could see were the handlebars, which had snagged some weeds. Chappy tried hooking them with a stick, but it was too short and he knew he'd have to go down, which meant getting his shoes and socks off and rolling up his pants legs. The bank was slippery and his feet sank in the ooze, making sucking sounds when he yanked himself free.

He tried to imagine Marcia actually taking Dody's bike, a heavy Schwinn with a chain guard and a decent headlight, but he couldn't get a picture of her. He saw the bike alone—as if steered by a ghost—pedals rotating, wheels spinning as it bumped across the stubble of the cottonfield, climbed the ditch road, and crashed over the edge into the water.

He hadn't ridden in years, so he had trouble at first, weaving like a drunk, once falling when he hit a rut and tearing his pants. The bike was too small so he pedaled with his knees out, like a Ringling clown, to avoid hitting the handlebars. As it was, he had to watch himself when he turned, or the pedal crank would plow into the ground and send him flying.

He rode for a long time before he started yelling, his voice ringing in the twilight. He was yelling about Dody and Elaine and the old man. He was yelling about Beverly and Mr. Hogan and what it was to be this way in 1963 and how the future would rise up and be gone too.

He was yelling because he knew why Marcia had stolen the bike. She loved him.

She loved him so much it hurt.

813.54 A132d
Abbott, Lee K.
Dreams of distant lives